Dear Readers,

We're so excited about our book series, Sprouse Bros. 47 R.O.N.I.N.! When we decided to develop a book series, we wanted to create stories kids our age would love. So we jam-packed our series with all of the cool things we love to read about—top secret plots, ninja fighters, ancient samurai weapons, and ultimate villains. We even have a lot in common with the main characters, Tom and Mitch, from our favorite desserts to our favorite bands. Because we love comics so much, we've included original comic-book style art—illustrated by an awesome comic book artist—in each book. We think it rocks, and we hope you do too!

Thanks for reading our series, and stay tuned for future episodes of Sprouse Bros. 47 R.O.N.I.N.!

Dylan Sprouse and Cole Sprouse

We would like to thank our dad,
Matt, and our manager, Josh, for
their constant support. Thanks
also to everyone at Dualstar and
Simon & Schuster for all of their
hard work. Last, but not least,
thanks to all of our friends and
fans—this is for you guys!
—Dylan Sprouse and Cole Sprouse

This book is a work of fiction. Any references to historical events, real people, or real locales are used fictitiously. Other names, characters, places, and incidents are the product of the author's imagination, and any resemblance to actual events or locales or persons, living or dead, is entirely coincidental.

SIMON SPOTLIGHT
An imprint of Simon & Schuster Children's Publishing Division • 1230 Avenue of the Americas, New York, New York 10020
Sprouse Bros.™ and related *Sprouse Bros.* trademarks are trademarks of DC Sprouse Inc., and licensed exclusively by Dualstar Entertainment Group, LLC. © 2008. DC Sprouse, Inc. All rights reserved, including the right of reproduction in whole or in part in any form.
SIMON SPOTLIGHT and colophon are registered trademarks of Simon & Schuster, Inc.
Manufactured in the United States of America • First Edition   10 9 8 7 6 5 4 3 2 1
ISBN-13: 978-1-4169-4784-4 • ISBN-10: 1-4169-4784-1
Library of Congress Catalog Card Number 2007933063

EPISODE #5 THE BETRAYAL

by Kevin Ryan
with Dylan Sprouse and Cole Sprouse
illustrated by Dan Panosian

MATTOON MIDDLE SCHOOL
MEDIA CENTER

Simon Spotlight
New York   London   Toronto   Sydney

Bad and good are intertwined like rope.
—*Japanese proverb*

PROLOGUE

Show-off, Mitch Hearn thought as his brother, Tom, launched at him with a series of strikes and high kicks. Mitch deflected them easily. But the attacks forced him backward and threw him off balance. Just before Mitch's back hit the wall, his brother let up.

Mitch didn't wait to see what Tom would do next. Instead Mitch bounced off the padded wall and then used the momentum to help him dive into a forward roll. He knew he needed to get out of Tom's reach to mount a successful counterattack.

Back on his feet, Mitch saw Tom coming out of his own roll. Because Tom favored high kicks and jumping attacks, he often found himself on the ground. As a result, he was very good at rolling or jumping back to attack position.

Mitch shook his head. This was going to be a long match.

"Enough!" a loud voice echoed through the chamber.

The boys stopped and faced each other, quietly panting. Their sensei circled them, sizing them up. When Mitch first met him, he'd expected to see a wizened, old Japanese man instead of an ordinary-looking, stocky white man of indeterminate age. Their sensei could have just as easily been a stockbroker, or an insurance salesman, or a high-school teacher. Of course, if you looked closely, you could see that he was very muscular under his black gi. And you might notice that he was always extremely alert and aware of his surroundings. He also had the fastest hands and feet that Mitch or Tom had ever seen.

Mitch guessed that their sensei had a name, but neither of the boys knew it. He was just Sensei.

"You are finished," their sensei said. Then he marched silently toward the right side of the octagonal room's padded walls, located the padded exit door, and disappeared through it.

Where was their lecture for the day? the boys wondered. It wasn't that they enjoyed being scolded and criticized; it was simply that they'd gotten used to it, and in their world surprises usually didn't end up being good.

"Um, what now?" Tom asked.

"No clue," replied Mitch. "Maybe he's coming back?" He looked up at the level above them where their butler, trainer, and cook, Mr. Chance, usually watched from behind a thick piece of glass. Today Mr. Chance was nowhere to be seen.

"Something isn't right here," Mitch said. Even as he said it, Tom ran over to the door. It was locked. That also had never happened before.

Mitch tried the door. It wouldn't budge.

"I didn't even know the door had a lock!" Tom said.

"Me neither. But it wasn't locked by accident, so the question is, why lock it *now*, when we're in here alone?" Mitch asked.

"Really?" Tom replied sarcastically. "'Cause I think the important question is how the heck do we get out?"

"That's a good one too," Mitch said. Something was wrong, seriously wrong.

Together, the boys stepped into the center of the room and looked up again at the glass above them on all sides. No one was there.

Suddenly two panels on the padded wall in front of

them flung open and two strange men entered the gym. Instinctively Mitch and Tom turned to stand back-to-back, to support each other and ensure that no one could attack either of them from behind. Mitch turned his head to see two other men appearing out of the wall on the other side of the gym. The four thugs eyed the brothers grimly.

"They don't look too friendly," Mitch muttered.

"No kidding," returned his brother.

The four men were wearing regular street clothes. They could have passed for street gang members, but Tom and Mitch had learned to be cautious; people are never what they seem.

Mitch was worried about Mr. Chance. Something must have happened to him. He was very rarely, if ever, away from their side. Was their sensei behind this? Had he captured Mr. Chance to get to them? Their clan, Cat's Claw, apparently had many enemies. Was he allied with one of them? Sure, Mr. Chance seemed to trust him, but could Mr. Chance have been wrong?

At once the men shrieked, high-pitched and in unison, and then they attacked.

Already in his defensive posture, Mitch blocked the first kick that came his way. But the men were strong and well trained. This wasn't going to be easy. He and Tom were skilled fighters. They had studied martial arts for years and had had over a month of Sensei's intensive workouts. Yes, they were skilled, they were quick, and they were young. But they were also outnumbered two to one.

For the first time, Mitch understood what it was like to truly fight for his life. What amazed him most was how calm he was. Remembering his training, he used his aikido and a few moves borrowed from other styles to deflect blows and keep on his feet. He knew that if he or Tom ended up on the ground, the fight would be over very quickly.

Mitch couldn't see his brother, but instead felt his movements from behind his back. And when one of the goons came charging at him, he used a simple hip throw to send the man flying backward toward Tom.

There was a loud grunt, and out of the corner of his eye Mitch saw the man lying on the floor. A moment later, another man stumbled into his striking range. It was a gift from Tom, and Mitch didn't waste it. He used a quick combination of elbow and hand strikes to put the man out.

Now it was two-on-two. The goons were wary and kept their distance.

"How you doing, Tom?" Mitch asked, breathing heavily.

"Pretty good, but I'm starved. What do you say we take out these bad guys and grab a burger?" said Tom.

"Sounds good. Then the quicker we do this, the quicker we eat," Mitch replied.

"You hear that, Mr. Bad Guy?" Tom said to the goon in front of him. "We're going to have to make this fast."

Without a signal, the boys attacked together, each picking the man closest to him. The suddenness of the attack put the men on the defensive. Mitch could see the hesitation in the eyes of his target. That was all he needed. Just one moment of hesitation, and Mitch used his opponent's weakness to his own advantage. A moment later the man was on the ground, unconscious.

Mitch turned to see his brother smiling, the last of the four attackers falling in a heap to the ground.

"I thought we were going to get a workout today," said Tom, dusting himself off.

Mitch shrugged. "I'm sure they did their best. Who were they, anyway?"

The moment the boys caught their breath, the door opened. Sensei and Mr. Chance stepped inside.

"Quiet!" Sensei said. Mitch automatically straightened up. Noticing Mr. Chance by their sensei's side, Mitch quickly discarded his theory that they had been betrayed. Instead it seemed that exactly the opposite was true: Mr. Chance was in on it.

"Students, this was a test and a challenge. We wished to challenge you in a contest where you believed you were in real danger," announced their sensei. "Unfortunately, your form was lousy, your discipline nonexistent, and the taunting of your opponents foolish." The silence was palpable. This was the lecture the brothers had been expecting. They prepared themselves for the worst. "But you did adequately," Sensei added finally as the men on the floor began to stir.

The boys' faces lit up.

"Can I just ask one question?" said Mitch.

Their sensei thought about it for a moment. "You may."

"When did you have that lock installed on the door?"

"Bad timing for a joke, bro," Tom whispered. "But it was a good one."

Their sensei glared at him, yet continued without acknowledging the disrespect. "I also wished to test how well you work together. And as sloppy as your fighting was, it seems you work very well as a team. This is a great strength. But one day your enemies might use it against you."

Before the brothers had time to process this warning, their sensei dismissed them. "That is all for today."

"Come," Mr. Chance said, and they all stepped outside and onto the streets of Tokyo.

"What did he mean by that?" Mitch wondered aloud.

"Yeah, how can our enemies use our teamwork against us?" said Tom.

Mr. Chance was thoughtful for a moment. "Working together more than doubles your strength," he said. "However, if you are ever both captured, they will use your bond against you. Your greatest strength will become your greatest weakness."

Mitch understood. "You mean if we are interrogated?"

"What do we do if we're captured by someone from Black Lotus?" Tom asked. Mitch thought Mr. Chance flinched at that question. "Can you teach us to resist?"

"Yes, but at the hands of a skilled interrogator, even the strongest in body and spirit will break. And Julian Vane and his Black Lotus ninjas are *very* skilled interrogators," Mr. Chance said.

"So what do we do if we are caught?" Mitch asked.

"Do not get caught," replied Mr. Chance.

"But what if we do?" Tom insisted.

For a moment Mitch saw that Mr. Chance was actually uncomfortable, which was rare.

"I am very serious. Do not get caught. I would not wish such a fate on even an enemy," Mr. Chance said.

"So what you're saying is, we shouldn't get caught?" said Tom, grinning.

Mr. Chance was not in a joking mood. "Do not get caught," he repeated gruffly.

CHAPTER 1

VANE ISLAND, PACIFIC OCEAN—PRESENT DAY

Tom couldn't keep silent. He knocked into his brother with his shoulder—a necessity because his hands were tied behind his back. "So what part of 'don't get caught' didn't you understand?"

"What?" Mitch said.

"Don't you remember anything Mr. Chance taught us? Rule number one: Don't get caught."

"Look, this is the best way to get to Julian Vane," said Mitch. He was calm, which drove Tom crazy.

"Yes, we'll get to him all right, but then he'll have his goons torture and kill us," Tom retorted.

"Look, if you have a better idea . . ."

"*Now* you ask me. Ten minutes ago you were Mr. Let's Surrender. Now you want to talk about it?" Tom said.

"Actually," Mitch began, "I changed my mind. I don't want to talk about it, so how about—"

"Well, we're *going* to talk about it. We're going to talk about how—"

A jolt to his back made him pause midsentence. Someone had shoved him from behind. "Keep it down!" yelled a Black Lotus ninja. Vane's ninjas wore loose-fitting, dark karate robes and dark scarves covering their heads and most of their faces. There were at least a dozen of these goons behind them.

Turning back to his brother, Mitch caught Laura Ting's eye. She also had her hands tied behind her back; two of the ninjas were pushing her forward roughly. Like the brothers, Laura was fifteen. Of slim build and medium height, she wore her long black hair in a ponytail. At the moment, her usually expressive face was locked into a scowl.

Mitch could tell that Laura looked scared, which was unusual for her. She was a spitfire; the first time he and Tom had ever seen a Black Lotus ninja, it was Laura who had come to their rescue. Still, now that they were captured, their future was in Vane's hands, and that would scare anyone. He knew exactly how she felt.

"Look, surrendering worked for Luke in the last movie. That's how he got to the emperor," Mitch whispered to Tom.

"A great film, don't get me wrong, but ARE YOU KIDDING ME? That *can't* be your plan!" Tom said.

"Why not?" asked Mitch.

"First of all, it's a *movie*! Secondly, don't you remember what happened?"

Mitch shrugged. "They got the bad guys . . . killed the emperor."

"Oh, sure. Luke got his butt kicked, and Darth Vader and Han had to do all the work," Tom said.

His brother looked deflated. "Oh, yeah." Brightening, he said, "Look, Mr. Chance is out there somewhere, the three of us are together, and we still have our training. This isn't over, not by a long shot."

"I'm just saying," Tom snapped, frustrated, "that there *has* to be a better way."

Ninjas shoved both Tom and Mitch, hard, from behind. The three prisoners knocked into one another one by one, like dominoes. "I said shut up!" one of the goons yelled. "Just keep walking."

They had been walking for about a quarter of a mile when Julian Vane's control center first came into view, rising up out of the jungle floor. It was monstrously large, designed to look like the Space Needle in Seattle—a giant flying saucer sitting atop a tall post. It must have been forty or fifty stories high. Beyond the tower, an even taller and more imposing mountain, which Mitch knew was an actual volcano, rose up from the horizon.

Finally, they arrived at the base of Vane's tower.

The bottom was made up of a massive circular slab of concrete, from which grew the cylindrical center support beam, solid as the trunk of a tree but twice the size.

They marched until they reached a row of glass doors. The ninjas halted abruptly, shoving the three captured teenagers closer together and surrounding them.

"You guys have a plan, right?" Laura whispered to her friends.

"Oh, absolutely," replied Mitch.

Tom knew what Mitch was doing. It wouldn't help for Laura to know just how much trouble they were in. Better to give her some hope. "Yes, just wait for our signal," he added.

She seemed relieved, and then they were moving again. A few seconds later they were inside a vast, open lobby. The interior was breathtaking; high ceilings, granite floors, and art deco furniture. It was almost easy to forget this building existed on an island in the middle of the ocean, and not on Fifth Avenue in New York City. There were life-size abstract murals on the walls and an odd-looking sculpture of a broken circle in the middle of the room. Tom didn't know much about modern art, but one thing he did know was that it had probably cost Vane a pretty penny.

A man in a business suit approached them, suspiciously eyeing the teenagers.

"Right this way," he said sternly, leading them toward the bank of elevators to the right. Like a member of the secret service, the man didn't seem to remember what a smile looked like.

There were four elevators, each operating between different sets of floors. All the doors were ajar, waiting to invite them inside. Then, just before one set of doors came to a close, two ninjas forced Laura into the elevator, and she disappeared behind the mirrored doors.

"Hey!" both boys protested at once, struggling to break free from their captors. They couldn't let them take her. They couldn't afford to be separated, not now!

Suddenly, four pairs of hands grabbed Tom and shoved him into a different elevator—and pushed his brother in as well, thankfully. "Enough," the man in the business suit commanded as he joined them inside.

Tom continued struggling tirelessly all the way up, until another jolt to his lower back made him wince in agony. He would have sunk to his knees if the ninjas hadn't been holding him up.

The elevator operated as smoothly and speedily as the one at the Matsu School. Tom would have given anything to be riding up in that one instead. After a remarkably short trip, the doors slid open and the boys were forced out and into a large room. "Wait here. Mr. Vane will come to deal with you personally," the man in the suit said.

After disposing of the brothers, Vane's goons disappeared back into the elevator, and Tom and Mitch realized that their hands were now free. Tom hit the button for the elevator. It didn't light up and the elevator didn't come.

"I'm sure it has a code," said Mitch.

"What now?" Tom said, but Mitch was too mesmerized by his surroundings to answer. The elevator had opened out into the center of the room. It seemed as though the elevator was the only way in or out, except for the windows that lined the room from floor to ceiling. The whole top floor of the building was one large circular room; half of the floor looked like it was meant for entertaining, furnished with smooth leather couches, glass coffee tables, and walls lined with high-definition television screens, including the largest one that either of them had ever seen. The other half of the floor was meant to function as an office, or so it seemed. Desks were cluttered with numerous computers and other high-tech equipment, only some of which Mitch recognized. In the center of the room was a massive conference table.

"We don't have much time," Tom said.

Mitch nodded. "Vane will be here soon."

"What do we do?"

"Well, I don't know. But whatever happens, we tell him nothing, we give him nothing, agreed? But we have to be ready. He'll probably try to use us against each other, like Mr. Chance said."

"I know, but, Mitch," Tom said, "I want you to know that no matter what they do to you, I won't talk and I won't give in."

"Um, good," said Mitch. "I think."

"No, I mean it. They could get really creative with the beatings and who knows what else. I don't care what they put you through, but I promise you," Tom said, smiling, "Vane will get nothing from me."

Mitch smiled back. "I only hope I get to return the favor when your turn comes, bro."

"Thank you," Tom replied, pausing to think about his possible punishments. "Or, you know, we could just escape and skip the whole torture routine."

"That's just what I was thinking. Let's look around."

The brothers circled the huge . . . what was it? Tom wondered. An office? A control center? Anything was possible. They just stood there, staring at the monstrous flat-panel television screen mounted on one of the walls.

"Must be a prototype," he said. "It's got to be at least a hundred inches."

Mitch broke his stare and instead eyed the row of monitors lined up on one of the desks. He jetted toward one. "Computer terminal. I wonder if I can access Vane's mainframe and network."

"Probably not. I'm sure Vane's got this place and his network booby-trapped ten million different ways," Tom replied.

He watched as Mitch's fingers raced over a keyboard. He heard his brother mutter under his breath. As time went on, the muttering got angrier and angrier.

"I'm right, aren't I?" asked Tom knowingly. This was one of the first times he wasn't so happy about being right.

"Passwords on everything," Mitch replied. "We're locked out. I can't even access read-only files or the net."

"Can't you just hack into it?" Tom cried.

"Of course I can, but I'd need hours to do it. Hours we don't have. I'll do what I can to crack some of these codes, but I don't know how far I'm gonna get before—"

All of a sudden they heard a loud beep coming from the elevator. Without a word, the brothers skidded back toward the elevator doors to see who was coming and prepare their attack. Just as the boys' feet screeched to a halt, the elevator doors opened and revealed three women. For a moment Tom was too stunned to say anything or even move.

The women, all in their early or mid-twenties, wore short silk robes and high-heeled sandals. Whoever they were, they clearly weren't who Tom and Mitch were expecting. They looked more like models. The first woman was blond-haired and blue-eyed; the next girl was Asian, with dark skin and long, dark, straight hair; and the third had a china-doll complexion with flowing, red, curly locks. All of them were beautiful.

Smiling sweetly, the women stepped off the elevator. Together the boys stormed the now empty elevator just in time to watch the doors separate them from the gorgeous models on the other side. Tom slammed the button marked G.

"What if they're waiting for us when we get to the bottom?" Mitch asked.

"We'll deal with it if it happens," said Tom. Anything was better than just waiting for the worst.

"We're not moving," Mitch said.

His brother was right. Tom hit the button again, and again, and again. The elevator didn't budge.

"Look." Mitch pointed to a small keypad with a screen above it that read PLEASE ENTER CODE. "Perfect," he said.

Tom hit the door open button. This one worked. "It looks like we're stuck here, at least until we can figure something out," he said.

The elevator doors slid open again and the three women reappeared, holding trays with bottles of soda, snacks, and chips.

"Mr. Vane ask us to take care of you until he arrive," the blond woman said. Her accent was thick and recognizably Russian. She spoke in broken English that made the boys wonder exactly how new she was to American employment.

Tom found that his mouth wouldn't work.

"Funny, they don't *look* like Vane's goons," Mitch said, nudging him.

"Obviously," mused Tom, "Vane has goons in all shapes and sizes."

"We can't trust them," Mitch warned.

"We could give them a chance. . . ." Tom saw his brother's sharp look and went on, "Of course not . . . but maybe if we play along . . ."

"We can get some useful information?" Mitch finished for him.

"Come, sit with us. Make yourselves comfortable," the woman with the Russian accent said.

Tom glanced at his brother and nodded, and both boys stepped out from the elevator and back into the glass office.

CHAPTER 2

Laura's room was small and empty. Parched, she considered banging on the door and asking for a drink of water, but she didn't. She refused to ask these people for anything.

After what felt like forever, Laura finally heard some noise in the corridor. She got into a fighting stance as the door opened. Four robed ninjas were waiting to greet her in the hallway. For a moment she contemplated attacking them. She might not win, but at least she would be doing something.

"Are we going to do this the hard way?" one of the ninjas asked.

Laura considered that—doing it the hard way. It would feel good to try, even if she lost, which was probably what would happen. Laura wasn't afraid to get dirty, and she wasn't afraid to get hurt. One thought stopped her: The boys might need her. Did Vane already have them in his custody? Were they suffering in a dark room, getting beaten—or worse?

Whatever small chance the three teenagers had, she knew, depended on them working together. And right now they were separated. She had to wait for an opportunity to do the boys and herself some real good until she could find them.

Relaxing her stance, she took a step back.

A pair of hands grabbed each arm, leading her out of the room and down the hall toward the elevator bank up ahead. It took all her will to keep calm, to not react. She reminded herself that the boys needed her; she was sure of it, and they must be struggling to be brave as well. She had seen it in their faces outside, when they told her they had a plan.

It was just to make her feel better, she knew. But the funny thing was that it did. Even if you have no courage, act as if you do. Most people cannot tell the difference, her father had said.

Her father.

He needed her too. At that thought, a surge of courage shot through her, and she knew she was doing the right thing. Laura felt ready for anything as she got into the elevator. After a short trip, they reached their destination. The flashing button on the panel told her they were at the top floor.

Last stop, she thought, preparing herself.

She heard gunfire. For a second she wondered if that was really what she heard, or if it was just firecrackers. The ninjas next to her didn't react. Maybe she was mistaken. Maybe it was her imagination.

There it was again, and this time it was clear.

Were her friends in trouble? Were they fighting for their lives? It took no more than a second, but it felt like an eternity passed before the elevator doors opened.

She took in her surroundings, noticing the large circular office and the floor-to-ceiling windows. She scanned the area, frantically looking for any sign of the boys. Then she heard it, more gunfire. This time it was so harsh she felt vibrations through the floor. It was coming from the other side of the office. Unfortunately that area was out of sight because of the elevator bank in the center of the room blocking her view. But she heard danger loud and clear.

Laura knew she should be careful, but there just wasn't time to think of herself. She simply ran toward the noise. What she saw on the other side stopped her cold in her tracks. For a moment her mind rejected the information. It had to be some strange trick of Vane's.

Laura blinked—she couldn't believe her eyes—but when she opened them she was staring at the same scene. On the plus side, the gunfire wasn't real. The sound that was booming through the room was coming from a very realistic video game being played on a giant screen. That should have made Laura feel relief. But it only made her angry.

The brothers were safe, all right. Facing away from her, they were stretched out on a big, comfy leather couch playing the video game. The three girls hovering over the boys looked up at her as she entered, smiling pleasantly. One of them held a can of soda to Tom's mouth so he could sip through a straw while he played. Another was handing Mitch snacks while he shouted at the giant screen.

Laura was too stunned to speak. Finally she walked around to the other side of the couch so they could see her glaring at them, her hands on her hips. It took a few seconds for them to register that she was even there.

At last they glanced her way. Barely taking their eyes off the screen, they said in unison, "Hey."

Hey? That's all they have to say for themselves? she thought.

Laura exploded. "ARE YOU KIDDING ME?" she yelled. That startled them out of their trance. Looking embarrassed, they dropped their game controllers and stood up.

"I thought you were dead!" Laura continued. "Or dying! Or getting tortured! And you were . . . I can't believe it, you were . . . you are . . . are you kidding me?" She was so mad she couldn't even get the words out without sputtering.

The three young women backed away gingerly, clearly not wanting to have any part of this. The boys also looked as if they would prefer to be somewhere else . . . anywhere else . . . perhaps even in Vane's clutches.

"We can explain," Tom protested meekly.

"This isn't what it looks like," added Mitch.

"Huh. Interesting. Because it looks like you are playing video games in Vane's fancy suite here with your new . . . um, friends, without the slightest regard or concern for what could have been happening to me!" She couldn't stop shouting. She tried to catch her breath. Forcing herself to calm down, she counted quietly to ten and then calmly said, "Well?"

"Okay, it *is* what it looks like, but we can still explain," Mitch said.

"Oh, I'd love to hear it. While you're at it, tell me about your great plan. Or should I wait for your signal? Maybe I could come back later? You could just have one of your *new friends* call when you need me," Laura said.

She wasn't surprised when the boys didn't respond. They just sat there, looking sheepish. Well, they had plenty to be sheepish about.

"Am I interrupting anything?" a smooth, deep voice said from behind her.

Laura spun around to see Julian Vane standing in front of them, smiling. He was quite impressive-looking in person. A tall man, with broad shoulders and dark, cool eyes that opened wide but still managed to hide many secrets. Under his expensive suit he had the physique of a bodybuilder. And she supposed he was handsome in a bland, news-anchorman sort of way. Of course, she didn't think much of the tall, dark, and evil type.

Vane nodded at them. "Tom and Mitch Hearn. Laura Ting, I'm so glad to finally meet you."

"I'll bet you are," Laura said, continuing to take her anger out on Vane, though truth be told, he certainly deserved it more than the boys did.

"What do you want from us?" said Tom, an edge to his voice. Laura was glad to hear that. It reminded her that she and the boys were still on the same side: against Vane.

"First, let me apologize to you, Laura. I'm sorry for the way you were treated. My staff misunderstood my orders.

You should have stayed with your . . . friends. Can I get you something? You must be thirsty. Or hungry?" he asked pleasantly.

"No, no, and no," Laura answered. "I don't want anything from you."

"I understand," said Vane. "But I do hope to eventually change your mind."

"Not very likely," Mitch chimed in. "You had your goons attack us and bring us here against our will, not to mention all the other damage you've caused."

Vane nodded. "True, but you *were* trespassing."

"Trespassing?" Mitch said.

"This is my island. It is my home and my place of business, and because of a loophole in international law, my own country. Yes, you were trespassing, and I was within my rights to detain you. I chose to exercise these rights in an effort to get us here together. I know what you three think of me—"

"You mean that you head up the Black Lotus gang? Yeah, we know all about you and what you've been up to, so you can stop trying to play us. Game over," said Mitch.

Vane smiled. "Mitch, you are the cautious one, thoughtful and rational, right? And Tom, you are the strong, rash one?"

"Actually, most people think of me as the good-looking

one," Tom said, with a smirk on his face.

Mitch shoved him. Vane laughed out loud.

"Yes, I know something about all of you. But you know, most of what you think you know about me is wrong."

"So you're *not* the leader of the Black Lotus gang?" Laura said.

"*Gang* . . . I prefer the term *Clan*," said Vane. "Not much different from the Cat's Claw Clan." He studied the boys' reactions, and then focused on Laura. "Or the Clan of the White Crane. Right, Laura?"

She swirled away from his mocking gaze.

"Sure, we're all exactly the same," Tom said. "We should throw a big pool party and barbecue to celebrate."

"But first, how about if you just release our fathers and all the other prisoners you're holding?" asked Mitch. "That way they can help carry the hot dogs and buns."

"I'm truly sorry about your fathers," Vane told them. "I assure you I had nothing to do with their disappearances." Before Laura could call him a liar, he raised his hands, as if in surrender. "Just hear me out."

"Why?" she snapped. "Why should we trust you?"

"Because I'm telling the truth, and I just want to talk to you. I sent my people away and I'm here alone." He looked over at the three ladies languishing nearby.

"Except for my able assistants over there, who are leaving." He smiled, and the ladies stepped into the elevator. "Though I am pretty good in a fight, there are three of you. I came alone because I wanted to show you that I'm sincere. After you've heard what I have to say, you can make up your own minds."

Laura couldn't believe her ears. She seriously thought about jumping Vane right there and then.

"And if we don't like what we hear, we can just go?" Mitch said.

"Yes, of course—"

"We don't like what we're hearing," said Laura, her teeth clenched. "Let's go."

Vane put on his reasonable face. "I'm not who you think I am; I'm not a monster. Look, I've made another gesture of goodwill." Vane led them to one of the windows, the one pointing to the east side of the island. They could see the inlet where the hulks of half-sunken ships lay. Next to the inlet was a small dock area. The *Rakurai* was docked there. Even at a great distance, Laura recognized the large hydrofoil ship. It looked like a large, fast yacht. In fact it was likely the fastest ship of its size in the world. The two-hundred-foot vessel sat on twin pylons that allowed it to practically fly across the surface of the water.

"I had your ship towed off the reef. My people are

working on it now," Vane said. He shook his head at the skeptical scowl on Laura's face and gestured to a telescope on a tripod nearby. "Take a look."

Mitch looked into the scope and said, "Okay, you have some people out there. So what? Big deal. They could be sabotaging the ship right now as we watch."

"If that were my goal, why the elaborate trick?" said Vane. He was being so patient. "I could have sunk it with the others. It would have been just one more vessel in the graveyard of unfortunates. Now, I've really gone out of my way to earn your trust and five minutes of your time. Are you ready to listen?"

The boys looked at each other and then at Laura's disapproving face. "Laura, it won't hurt to listen," Tom said.

"Yeah, let's just hear him out," Mitch agreed.

Laura couldn't believe what was happening. This was so obviously a trick. The boys had been playing video games too long. Their brains had gone soft. Why were they being so easily swayed? She sighed. The three of them needed to stick together if there was to be any hope of getting out of this alive. And one thing was for sure, they would get *nowhere* if they trusted Vane. Why couldn't the boys see it?

Reluctantly she followed the group to the large conference table and took a seat.

CHAPTER 3

Vane leaned forward and lowered his voice to almost a whisper, as if he were letting them in on a secret. "The feud between our clans happened so long ago that no one remembers how or why it started," he said. "Since then, we've been on different paths."

"Yeah, good and evil," Laura retorted. "We know all about the things you've stolen, the companies you've ruined, the people you've hurt and captured to make a profit."

Vane smiled. "I'm a businessman, and a very good one at that. I make no apologies for buying and selling. But I've never stolen from anyone, not a dime. I don't need to, and more importantly, it would violate my code and my clan's code of ethics."

"Code of ethics? You've *got* to be kidding me," said Laura. "You stole two of my father's inventions! Your whole business is built on theft."

Vane shook his head. "Your father and I made a legal

and binding agreement years ago. It's true, I got the better half of the arrangement, and I always regretted—"

"You *regretted*!" she shouted.

"I tried to make amends with your father recently, partly because of this new threat we all face. Frankly, I need his help, as I need your father's help," he said, glancing at the boys. "And I want you to know," he continued, glancing back at Laura, "that I had nothing to do with the recent attempts to take his new processor, though I know who was behind them. I dismissed Roman Maldeen from my service years ago; he was not working under my orders, despite what he may have told you. And I had nothing to do with the disappearance of either of your fathers or anyone else. I mean that sincerely."

"That's ridiculous," said Laura. "You think you can just make up some story about a phony legal agreement and I'll believe *you* over my own father, just like that? That I could possibly think that *he's* the liar, not you?"

"Ah, well, I'd rather not use such strong and negative terms, but allow me to put forth a small bit of evidence for my case: This isn't the first time your father has lied to you. Both of your fathers have lied to you, have they not? When was it again that you first learned about their secret identities? I wonder why they didn't have the decency to tell you themselves. . . ."

"That's it. Let's go," Laura said, glancing at her friends.

"Ms. Ting, I apologize for the blunt delivery, but what I said is true. It's not the first time you have been deceived by him. But I'm not here to convince you that your father is a liar. I'm simply here to show you that *I* am not one. Your father runs a successful computer business, which hinges on the notion that other local businesses must fail. And Mitch and Tom, your father is successful, isn't he? *Very* successful."

"They use their money to do good," Mitch said. Of course he didn't really know anything about what his father did with the money he made, and Vane was right about one thing at least: Their father had certainly been keeping a lot of secrets from them. But Mitch was determined to prove a point, no matter what.

"Well, I personally see to it that much of the money I make goes to good causes as well," said Vane. When Laura grunted, he went on, "Do you know what the leading cause of death in Africa is? Malaria. Millions a year. More than all other diseases combined. But because of Vane Enterprises' clean water program, there will be a lot fewer deaths next year, and fewer still the year after that. We do make money. We compete fairly and we win more than we lose. It's called staying in business. And then we try to give something back."

"Tell me, what exactly were you planning on giving back after you hijacked the world's nuclear reactors?"

Laura demanded. "You're not fooling anyone with this act, Mr. Vane." However, she saw the brothers listening intently. She wondered if maybe they *were* being fooled. Big-screen televisions, beautiful women waiting on them, and now this story about helping the poor. Were they actually buying it? The image of the modern-day Robin Hood that Vane was painting of himself?

"You are very clever, Laura," said Vane, smiling so pleasantly. "But you see only a small part of the big picture. Your vision of the world is incomplete, just like the bits and pieces of information you have about me. Therefore, the conclusions you draw are incorrect. It's true I collected information about nuclear reactors, but as part of an effort to *protect* them from the real threat, not hijack them for my own purposes." He watched her roll her eyes and knew he would have to give her more. "It is very easy to blame everything on me, to convince yourself that you finally have the enemy within your reach, but that would be yet another false conclusion. However, you are right in concluding that there are terrorists out there working right now to destroy everything you hold dear. They want to destroy everything and everyone you love.

"You may think of me as a heartless corporate pirate, but even if that were true, that doesn't make me a terrorist. Because my business interests are so varied,

I sometimes have to get involved in security matters that might affect a certain leg of my business. These security matters sometimes make me privy to otherwise classified information. I recently discovered that the world's reactors were vulnerable to cyberattack. At that point I connected with Mr. Matsu, and the two of us, with the help of the powerful technology that Matsu Cybernetics could offer, intended to eliminate that vulnerability. That is, until you three stepped in, with more incomplete information, and sabotaged everything. In fact, thanks to your work, the terrorist threat is still at large."

"Okay, let's say we believe you," Mitch said, holding up a hand to silence a fuming Laura. "What do you want from us?"

"That's simple. Help. You three are obviously intelligent, and you are clearly a very strong team. Working with all the information, not just bits and pieces, together we can stop them. I think I may even be able to help you find your fathers. With all three clans working together, we can put a stop to a very dangerous terrorist organization once and for all." Vane smiled.

"I don't like what I'm hearing," Laura said pointedly.

Vane nodded. "You're young; you can afford to have a naive view of the world. But when you get older, you see that the world is more complex than you realize.

Good and bad are not always black-and-white. The world is shades of gray, my young friends."

"We'd like to think about it," said Mitch.

"Of course," Vane said. "Take some time, but remember that we have to move quickly." He got up.

"And some say you're just a big, dumb bully," Tom said.

Something flashed in Vane's dark, cool eyes. Laura noticed a wince; Vane didn't like being called names. Then it passed. A second later he was all smiles again and headed for the door, waving to them politely as he left.

"So?" Mitch said. "What do you guys think?"

"I think," replied Laura, "he's a lying snake."

"How much do we really know about him?" Tom said. "He could've killed us by now if he wanted to."

"You can't be serious!" Laura cried, feeling like she'd walked into a nightmare.

"No, I mean it. He really *could* have killed us by now."

"Tom's right, Laura," said Mitch. "Calm down. We have to at least think about what Vane told us."

Tom smiled. "You know how I do my best thinking?"

"It's how I do *my* best thinking." The brothers headed for the large screen and turned on the video game.

This can't be happening, Laura thought. Somehow she felt worse than she had when they'd been captured and she was sure they were all facing death. At least they had been in it together. Now . . . now it seemed like her whole world was falling apart. She couldn't figure out anything anymore.

As Laura watched Tom and Mitch manipulating the controllers in their tense hands, she felt nothing but sadness. Whatever happened, she would have to go on alone. And to imagine that she'd thought . . .

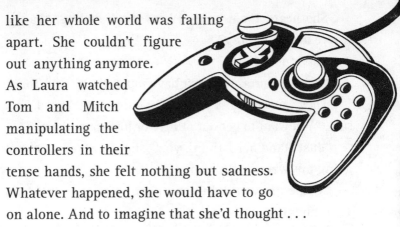

Well, she didn't know what she had thought. But now she knew one thing for sure. If she got another chance at Vane, she wouldn't waste it.

Not even bothering to tell them where she was going, Laura headed for the elevator. She'd wait, and when Vane appeared she would strike. He was bigger and no doubt had more training than she did. But whatever she lacked in size and experience, she made up for in pure rage. She looked over her shoulder; Tom was engrossed in the game. Meanwhile Mitch was adjusting the volume on what looked like a complicated stereo.

She made her way to the elevator door, still hearing the stupid game and shouting from the boys.

Then silence.

She refused to even think about them. She was done with the Brothers Hearn. Ugh.

She heard them behind her, Mitch calling, "Laura, where are you going?"

She ignored him.

"Really, Laura, we don't have much time," said Tom.

They came to flank her. She stared straight ahead. Tom said, "You want to get out of here or just stand there?"

"Just stand here, thank you," she answered. "I'm not going anywhere with either of you."

"Come on, you didn't think we were serious?" said Tom, nudging her.

"Keep your shoulders to yourself," said Laura.

"We had to make it look good until we could fry his bugs," Mitch explained.

"Fry his *whats*?"

"Listening devices. Hidden microphones. We used the sound on the game to fry them. I tuned the equalization on the stereo for maximum output on certain . . . You know what?" Mitch said. "We don't have time for this. Vane will be back as soon as he realizes he can't hear us talking. We have to go."

Laura felt a weight lifting off her shoulders. "You mean you weren't fooled?"

"By Dr. Evil's lamebrain pitch?" said Tom, smiling.

For the first time since they'd been caught, Laura had to fight back tears. She didn't want them to think she was a girl—even though she was a girl. "When did you know? When you called him stupid? Did you see the look in his eyes?"

"I saw it—pretty *creepy*," said Tom. "But I knew when he first opened his big, fat mouth."

"All part of the plan," Mitch said.

"Does the plan include a way out of here?"

"I'm glad you asked," Tom said. "As a matter of fact, it does. Follow me."

He motioned them into the elevator and hit a code on the keypad. To Laura's surprise, the door closed and the elevator started moving.

"How did you do that?" she asked.

"I caught the code when the girls left," Tom told her. "While you were talking to Vane—" He fell silent when the elevator stopped abruptly. They had only gone down a few floors. He shrugged. "I hit the button for the ground level."

The door opened. Four men were standing there in black ninja gear. They looked at the teenagers in surprise, as if they were expecting someone else. Laura didn't hesitate; she gave a shout and charged, and felt her friends fall in line behind her.

Seeking out the biggest one, she attacked. Knowing Vane, Laura was sure these ninjas had both training and experience. She guessed that none of that experience included fighting a slim, seemingly innocent fifteen-year-old girl. Her target actually smiled when he saw her coming; his facial expression seemed to say, Oh, this one's going to be a piece of cake.

Laura enjoyed watching that smile fly off him as she struck the man with a series of hand blows, making solid contact on his face. He was still standing when she was done. Though stunned, he managed to mount his counterattack. That was what she was waiting for.

Stepping back, she waited as he rushed her. Deflecting blows, she leaned in and did a simple hip throw. His own size and momentum worked against him, and his head made solid contact with the wall.

When she turned, the other three men were on the ground and the boys were smiling. "I got two," Tom said.

"True, but mine was a head taller than either of them," Laura said, returning the smile. They were a team again. And though the odds were still against them, it felt like they at least had a fighting chance.

"Where are we?" Mitch wondered, scanning the area.

They walked down the short hallway and looked around. The hallway opened into a large, luxurious living room with yet another wide-screen television, and to the left was a spacious new kitchen with state-of-the-art appliances. Laura opened the door on her right and saw two beds with pink and purple bedding . . . and lace curtains.

"I think I know," she said.

"Where?" asked Tom, peeking inside. "Ew. Something purple threw up in there."

"Your girlfriends from upstairs, this is where they live," Laura guessed.

"They aren't exactly our friends," Tom said.

"Whatever," Laura replied. Just then Mitch spotted a computer on the desk in the corner of the living room and made a beeline for it.

"That's why the elevator code only took us here," Mitch realized. "The code they used must take them only to the apartment, nowhere else. You guys look for a way out, I have an idea." He got to work.

"I suppose this is all part of your plan?" Laura asked mockingly.

"Yup," said Mitch, already concentrating on the screen.

CHAPTER 4

Tom and Laura took a quick tour of the entire floor. It was more luxurious than anything they had ever seen, full of expensive furniture, art, and electronics. The closets were stuffed with designer clothes, hundreds of pairs of shoes, and glitzy jewelry.

"What good is all this junk?" Tom asked. "Where would they even wear those clothes, those diamond earrings?"

"They looked pretty dressed up when they were playing video games with you two," said Laura bitingly. Then she realized how truly sad their lives must be, locked up on this island, forced to do Vane's bidding. "But they can't go anywhere. They're prisoners. It's fancy, it's gilded, but it's a cage."

Tom opened another door and saw an oval Olympic-size swimming pool. A full gym lay beyond it. "I guess," he said. "But if you've got to live in a cage . . . I'm sure Vane's not *forcing* them to work for him."

"There are many types of 'force,'" said Laura.

"I don't even know what that means," Tom said. "Look, can we focus on finding a way out of here?"

"You're the one staring at the swimming pool," retorted Laura.

He went back to one of the bedrooms and tried a sliding glass door that led to a balcony. "Well, we know we can get outside."

"It's just a jump down fifty floors," Laura said.

"You first," said Tom. "Wait, I've got another idea." He pointed to a metal grate in the wall near the elevator at the center of the floor. The grate was about two feet square, just big enough to climb through.

"Something every building this size has to have," Tom noted. "Ventilation shafts." He pulled out his pocket pal and unfolded the screwdriver. "Watch and learn."

A moment later he removed the grate and saw that the passage was not a single two-foot-wide shaft, but four smaller ones bunched together. Each of them was much too small to crawl through.

"This is impossible," Tom protested. "But it worked in *Die Hard*."

"And *Mission Impossible* . . . and *Star Trek*," said Laura. "It looks like even bad guys go to the movies."

"But Mitch's *Star Wars* plan totally worked!"

"Do you have a backup plan?" Laura asked. "One

that you didn't steal from a screenplay?"

"As a matter of fact . . . ," said Tom. He pulled a curtain rod off the wall and used it to pry open the elevator door. The shaft was pretty big, and there was a ladder mounted on the side that led all the way down.

"It'll take a little while, but we can get down," Tom said. "Just pray that no one uses the elevator."

Laura looked impressed. "All right. Let's get Mitch."

They found him still at the computer. "Come on, bro," Tom told him. "We found a way out."

"No, can't leave yet," said Mitch.

"You can chat with your cyber-loser buddies at home," said Tom. "We want to live through the day."

"This computer didn't have a password," Mitch explained, still not getting up. "Vane gave them very limited access, but it's still connected to his network. They have access to the Internet."

"So?" asked Tom.

"So I can create a worm to attack his network and lock him out of his own system."

"What good will *that* do?" Laura said impatiently.

"Tick him off," answered Mitch, smiling.

"I love this plan," Tom said.

"I just need a little time," Mitch pleaded.

"How long?" said Laura.

"Fifteen minutes, maybe twenty," Mitch said. "I've

got to create a program to—"

"Do it. What do you need from us?" Laura interrupted.

"Just leave me alone. I'll work as fast as I can and then we'll get out of here."

"Feel like a snack?" Tom asked Laura.

"Actually, I do," she said. The kitchen had nothing but carrot sticks and salad. Laura grabbed a few carrots and a glass of water. Then they went back into the living room and continued pacing back and forth.

After twenty minutes, Mitch finally looked up. "Done. I even threw in a nice little surprise."

"Now let's focus on saving ourselves," said Tom.

They ran for the elevator. Tom grabbed the curtain rod and stepped toward the door.

Which was exactly when it opened.

Inside were the three women in short robes from Vane's office. The women looked at the goons on the floor, then up at the three teenagers. The redhead reached back into the elevator. Tom saw that she was going for the alarm button. He also saw that he would never be able to stop her in time.

"Wait!" Laura called out.

To Tom's surprise, the young woman actually did.

"We just want to talk to you," Laura continued.

"Mr. Vane will not be happy," she said in a thick Spanish accent.

"Mr. Vane is part of something terrible. We're here to stop him," explained Laura.

"Laura!" Mitch protested, afraid she had said too much.

"No, we have to trust them if we want their help," she said. Then she turned back to the women. "You know better than anyone who he really is. Help us."

"What you want from us?" asked the Russian lady.

"Don't sound any alarms, just give us a few minutes' head start . . . please," Laura said.

"Mr. Vane would be very angry with us if he knew we helped you," the Spanish woman pointed out.

"You only work for him, he doesn't own you. If we succeed, we're going to shut him down for good. You can get out of here and get back to your lives," said Laura.

The tension in the room was palpable as the silence bore on. The women stood still, staring at their supposed enemies, trying to decide their next move. If they were going to sound the alarm, wouldn't they have done it by now? Tom was surprised to see that the women seemed to be listening to Laura. Perhaps they really were being held against their will. He'd thought they were done for, but somehow Laura had managed to turn it around.

Just then the Spanish woman lunged backward into the elevator and pounded down on the alarm. The siren rang out and echoed through the entire floor. He was sure it was also ringing throughout the rest of the building.

The Asian woman stepped back into the elevator as well, but the blond Russian hesitated. The others didn't wait. The door closed and they disappeared.

"I think we're in trouble," Tom observed.

"I'm sure of it," Mitch said.

The woman nodded. "You don't have much time."

"Tom, if you can open the elevator door, we can buy ourselves a few minutes," said Mitch.

"I'm on it," Tom said, picking up the curtain rod. He pried open the door. With Mitch's help, he set the rod to prop open the door so the automatic safety system wouldn't allow the elevator to reach the floor. Vane's goons would have to climb the ladder to get to them.

"So what now?" asked Laura.

"Actually, I'm open to ideas," Mitch said.

"There's another way down," the woman told them.

"Great. How?" Tom asked.

"If I help you, you take me with you?" she said.

"Listen, no offense, but you girls kind of failed my whole trustworthy test," said Laura.

"I did not. I am still here. If you not help me, I not help you," she countered.

"You've got a point," Mitch interjected. "Okay, you're coming with us. What do we do?"

The woman disappeared around the corner and came back with four parachutes.

"I like this plan," Tom said, picking up a parachute and strapping it on. Everyone else followed suit.

"Mr. Vane keeps them on every floor, for escape," the woman said.

"Thank you . . . uh, what's your name?" asked Tom.

"Nadia."

"Thanks, Nadia. I'm Tom, that's my brother, Mitch, and that's Laura. Now let's get out of here," Tom said.

Just as they started to move, they heard a loud banging sound coming from outside. It reminded Tom of the chronic noisy construction work that took place outside their New York City brownstone, which, much like an alarm clock, woke them up at ungodly hours every morning, including Saturdays and Sundays. They all turned toward the window and saw huge metal bar shutters descend from the ceiling, slowly locking onto each of the windows, shutting the group inside. Again, Tom's mind floated back home, thinking about how similar these metal bars were to the gates that protected New York City storefronts at night. Zapping himself out of his reverie, he grabbed a metal chair, raced to the window, and propped the chair up under the closing shutter. It held at three feet off the ground.

"Get out there," he ordered everyone else, gesturing to the balcony.

They had to crouch down low, but they all managed to slip under the shutter. Then Tom noticed that the steel at the top of the chair was beginning to bend. He didn't wait to see what happened next, and instead slipped through himself just in time. As his right leg made it through the opening he heard a loud crash; the shutter smashed through the chair where Tom's leg had just been.

"Now comes the hard part—we jump," said Tom.

"Are we high enough?" Laura wondered.

"I'm not sure, but we don't have a choice," Tom said.

"We're five hundred and twenty-nine feet up, give or take," Mitch noted.

"How can you possibly know that?" asked Tom.

"Don't you remember when we visited the real Space Needle in Seattle with Dad? Didn't you read any of the little signs?" Mitch said.

"Dude, that was seven years ago. We were in second grade. How can you possibly remember that fact?"

"How can you—"

"Can you two not do this now?" Laura cut in. "You know, with the bad guys after us and all?"

Tom shook his head. "Right. Look, five hundred feet is okay, barely. What we're about to do is called BASE jumping. You have to pull the rip cord as soon as you clear the balcony. Then just enjoy the ride down."

"So you've done this before?" asked Nadia.

"Um . . . not exactly," Tom said.

The girls looked at him skeptically.

"It's not like we have much choice," said Tom. "Look, it'll be okay. Just point yourself east toward the *Rakurai* and follow me."

"No, we're not going to the ship," Mitch said.

"Why? Where else would we go?" asked Tom.

"You heard Vane in his lame pitch, this island is his own *country*. The perfect place for him to hide all his secrets, and all his prisoners . . ."

"Dad!" Tom cried with excitement, realizing at last how close they could be to getting him back.

"Maybe," replied Mitch. "And maybe Emiko, and your father, Laura, and others."

"Okay, but how do we know where he's keeping them? They could be anywhere on the island," Laura said.

"I have no idea. But there must be some kind of prison or some remote building that he uses for this kind of stuff. I'm sure these aren't the first people he's detained," Mitch said.

All three pairs of eyes turned to Nadia. "Do you know where Vane keeps his hostages?" Laura asked.

"It is not safe. Mr. Vane will be looking for us. He

will know that I help you," Nadia said. "We need to leave the island."

"He's captured our friends and our fathers," said Mitch.

"We're not leaving until we know for sure they're not here," Tom added.

Nadia sighed. "Okay, I can show you where the detention center is. He sends us to bring them food twice a day."

Tom nodded. "Okay, follow me down."

"Follow you?" asked Nadia.

"You can steer a little by pulling on the lines. Pull right to go right. Pull left to go left. If you hit the ground hard, roll." Tom wasn't worried about Mitch or Laura, but Nadia didn't exactly have their training. Unfortunately there wasn't much he could do about that now. As long as she pulled the cord, she'd get down in one piece.

They could hear noise on the other side of the steel shutters. It was time to jump.

Everyone spread out and stood on the railing. "We go on three. Keep your hand on the rip cord and pull it as soon as you're in the air." Tom wanted to show everyone how to use the reserve chute, but if someone's main chute didn't open immediately, there would be no second chance.

There was shouting coming from inside the building. And someone was banging on the steel.

"One," Tom said.

"Two," Mitch followed.

"Three," Laura finished.

Tom launched himself into the air, watching the others do the same. He pulled his cord and hoped for the best.

CHAPTER 5

Mitch felt a sharp tug upward as the chute opened. He looked down and saw that he was still at least two hundred feet off the ground. Then he looked around, counting three other open parachutes. They would all make it.

Pulling the lines on his right, Mitch steered toward the opening in the trees he had seen from above. The ground came up fast, faster than he had expected. He prepared to touch down when at the last second a gust of wind pulled his chute forward, forcing him to tumble with it. Mitch didn't fight the chute. Instead he rolled and came to a stop flat on his back.

A second later he saw a shadow hovering above him. "Trouble with the landing, bro?" Tom asked.

"No, why?" said Mitch, brushing the dirt off his legs and standing up. He unhooked himself from the chute and saw that Laura was doing the same. Mitch was about to offer Nadia help when he looked over and saw her standing there, already untangled from her parachute. Incredibly, her hair didn't even look messed up.

"Nadia, can you point us to the detention area?" Mitch asked.

"I take you there," she said.

"Actually, we'd rather you didn't," Laura told her. "Just point us in the right direction. It will be dangerous anyway."

"No, I go with you. That is agreement. I have help you so far. If Mr. Vane find me . . . *that* would be more dangerous," she said.

"Okay, you're with us," said Mitch. He could tell Laura wasn't happy, but she didn't argue.

"They'll be expecting us to try to escape right away, so that should buy us a little bit of time. And Vane probably doesn't know we know about the detention area yet," Tom said.

"Can I assume you have a plan, Captain?" Laura asked.

Mitch smiled. "Of course."

"Then let's stop wasting—," Tom began.

"Okay," interrupted Mitch. "Here's the *Rakurai* in the east," he announced, drawing a makeshift map in the sand with a stick. "We're here, in the middle, near Vane's Space Needle and the volcano to the north." He held out the stick. "Nadia," he said.

She drew an *X* on the east side of the island. "It's here."

"The plan is that we go in, get the prisoners out, and escape," Mitch stated.

Laura smiled. "Piece of cake."

"The island can't be more than two miles long by, maybe, a mile and a half wide. And there's plenty of tree cover, so they'll have to search for us on foot. That'll certainly buy us a bit more time. Let's get to the detention center and see what we're up against and we'll go from there."

Less than a second later, a loud alarm sounded. "ATTENTION. SELF-DESTRUCT SYSTEM ACTIVATED. ALL ISLAND PERSONNEL SHOULD EVACUATE IMMEDIATELY AND GO DIRECTLY TO THE DESIGNATED ESCAPE BOATS. THIS ISLAND WILL SELF-DESTRUCT IN NINETY MINUTES."

"They've *got* to be kidding!" Tom cried out.

"Self-destruct . . . ," said Mitch.

"This is bad," Nadia told the others. "Mr. Vane warn us about this. The island sits on a *vulkan*. How do you say again?"

"Volcano," Laura supplied.

"Yes, a volcano. And there are explosives . . . ," Nadia said.

"Wait a second. Did you set off the self-destruct when you were playing with the computer?" Tom asked his brother.

"No way! And I wasn't *playing* with the computer. I was cutting off Vane's access to his own network, remember?"

"You're sure you didn't accidentally hit the button to, I don't know . . . *destroy us all*?" Tom asked.

"No way, I'm sure of it," said Mitch. "Besides, if I had, we would have heard this message a long time ago."

"Look, you boys can fight later. We have a real problem here," Laura put in.

"Okay, new plan. We still go to the detention area, but now do everything much faster," Tom said.

"Nadia, lead on," ordered Mitch. The young woman took off at a trot—a pretty fast trot, actually. Mitch and Tom found themselves reaching their top speed pretty quickly in order to keep up. Laura didn't look happy, but she did the same.

As they moved through the jungle, Tom, Mitch, and Laura began to get winded. Nadia, who continued at her regular pace, had barely broken a sweat. I guess she used that gym quite a bit, Mitch thought as he increased his own speed. He caught Laura looking at Nadia with an expression that was somehow both surprised and annoyed at the same time.

The terrain of the jungle slowed them down a bit, but Nadia was able to lead them across the island in about fifteen minutes. At the other end, the jungle started to thin out as the ground grew rockier. Mitch knew this side of the island ended in rocky cliffs. He spied a series of low buildings. Most were made from brick and falling apart, and Mitch assumed these were from the war. In the center of the grounds, sticking out like a sore thumb, was a large, one-story concrete box. Actually, it looked more like a bunker.

Unlike the surrounding brick buildings, the large white cement rectangle had been built long after the war. The facility spanned hundreds of yards across. There were no windows, just a single steel door that served as its entrance and exit. Mitch spotted video camera towers on the roof; there was a station every hundred feet or so.

"Looks pretty secure," Tom said, crouching down beside him.

"What can you tell us about it, Nadia?" Mitch asked the Russian woman.

"It *is* secure. There is the video cameras, and there one door, six-inch stainless steel. The wall are steel, how you say . . . uh . . . reinforced concrete. Inside, two guards," said Nadia.

"Just two?" Tom asked.

"Yes, but with door locked, Vane don't need any more than that. No one can get in or out. Magnetic lock," she said.

"Have you seen the inside? Do you know who's in there?" Laura asked, tension in her voice. Mitch knew she was thinking the same thing he and Tom were thinking: My dad might be in there.

Nadia nodded. "There are ten cells, no windows, no bars—just solid steel doors. The prisoners cannot see or hear each other." Then, before anyone could speak, she added, "He did not tell us who is here, just that they are important . . . part of some great plan. He like to brag, but he never tell us anything important."

"Look, I hate to be a downer, but we don't have a lot of time here—what, ninety minutes?" said Mitch.

"THIS ISLAND WILL SELF-DESTRUCT IN SEVENTY MINUTES. ALL PERSONNEL TO THE DESIGNATED ESCAPE BOATS."

"Okay, make that seventy minutes," Mitch corrected himself.

"I'm sure Vane won't dare leave this island without collecting his prizes," Laura interjected. "And I bet he'll send more than two guards here to fetch them."

Tom shook his head. "So, let me get this straight: We've got an impregnable high-tech prison, but we have to break in somehow, rescue everybody inside, *and* get out before who knows how many of Vane's goons show up to destroy us? That is, unless the island does it first."

"Pretty much," Mitch replied. "That about covers it."

"Well, Mitch, have you got a plan for this one?" Tom pressed.

"I was thinking we could take turns," said Mitch.

"Great. What does that mean?" Laura said.

The three teenagers stared at one another. All their training, everything they had done so far . . . and none of it compared to what they now had to face. Their dads might be inside that building, and this rescue mission was all they had. Either they would succeed and save their friends and fathers from doom, or they would all suffer the same horrifying fate.

Mitch felt the seconds ticking away.

Finally a voice broke the silence. "I think I can help you," said Nadia.

The other three turned their heads in surprise.

"I think I have a . . . plan."

CHAPTER 6

Nadia walked down the path that led straight to the only entrance to Vane's private prison. She smiled and waved at the cameras near the door. That was their cue. Tom, Mitch, and Laura ran back through the jungle, circled back around, and took cover inside one of the old brick buildings nearest the front entrance of the prison. The place was falling apart; its wooden roof was rotted all the way through, and bricks were strewn all around.

Nadia had told them the older buildings dated back to World War II; the Japanese had used the island as a storage and transfer facility. The boys and Laura entered the building and navigated their way through piles of bricks and holes in the floor until they finally made it to the other side. They halted in front of a broken window and waited. From there, it was less than a hundred yards to the prison's front door, and they had a clear view ahead of them.

Nadia was in the doorway, talking to someone inside. Finally she stepped into the rectangular fortress.

That was their second cue. They were off. Tom led the way, kicking open the rotted-out door. He raced at full speed toward the steel door to the prison, with his brother and Laura close behind him. As he got closer, he could see inside the prison. He could see Nadia talking to one of Vane's ninja guards.

A second later Tom burst through the opening and came face-to-face with the second guard, who was sitting behind a console of controls and monitors. The man launched himself forward to hit the alarm button.

"Vane's coming!" Tom screamed, hoping this would buy him a few seconds. "He's right behind me!"

The ninja stopped moving, his hand barely touching the alarm button, and leaned over to look through the opening for Vane. Just then Tom launched himself into the air and struck the ninja with a flying kick to his chest. The man went down immediately, falling backward and crashing into the wall behind him.

Tom heard a commotion and turned around to see Laura standing over the other guard, who was also sprawled out and unconscious on the floor.

"A plan that works," Tom said. "Imagine that."

"Thanks, Nadia," Mitch chimed in.

"My pleasure," Nadia told them. "I hate these men.

They always rude to me when I come to bring the food."

Mitch sat down and looked over the security console. "Check the guards for key cards."

Tom quickly grabbed a card around his guard's neck. "Got it!" he said. Then Laura checked her guard and found another one. They headed down the hallway. Tom counted ten steel doors, five on each side.

Mitch looked up from the console. "I don't think any of them hit the alarm. And even if they did, it looks like the network is down," he said, smiling.

"Thanks to you, bro," said Tom.

"We gotta be quick," Mitch warned. Tom nodded in agreement. He could feel his heart pounding a mile a minute as they walked toward the cells; their dad might be behind any one of those doors. They stopped at the first one. There was no window, not so much as a handle. But he did see an electronic key reader, similar to a computerized door key reader in a hotel.

Mitch looked at the door and said, "Probably magnetic locks. And there's no keypad. I say we try swiping the cards at the same time."

Tom and Laura got into position as Mitch counted off.

"One. Two. Three."

They swiped the cards and immediately the door swung open, revealing a fairly large room. There was

furniture—a bed, a desk, and even a television—but no people. The walls were thick and padded, making them virtually soundproof. A soundtrack of classical music was playing in the background, loud enough to drown out any outside noise that might have made its way through the sound-resistant technology. The boys discerned that this music was probably blaring in every cell in the facility to ensure complete and total alienation and secrecy of the prisoners. Farther inside the cell, the boys found an empty closet and a small bathroom.

At the next cell, they were disappointed again. Finally, when the door of the third cell was flung open, they found an Asian man whom they did not recognize.

But someone else did.

"Daddy!" Laura cried out excitedly.

"Laura," said the man, his face a mixture of happiness and concern. "What are you doing here?" Then he looked at Tom and Mitch and said, "Wait, I know you."

"We're Jack Hearn's

boys," Mitch told him, smiling proudly.

"Yes, we have never met but I have seen you in pictures. You father is very proud of you," said Mr. Ting.

"Is he here?" Tom asked.

"I do not know. I have seen no one but Vane and his people," Mr. Ting said.

"Laura, give me your card and fill your dad in," said Mitch. Then Tom and Mitch tried the next door. There was another unrecognizable Asian man inside.

"Who are you?" the man asked, not sure whether to trust them or knock them out.

"We'll be your rescuers for today," Tom said.

Then Mr. Ting appeared next to him. "It is good to see you, Inoshiro," Mr. Ting greeted the man.

"And you," the stranger replied pleasantly.

"This is Mr. Inoshiro Matsu," Mr. Ting explained to the rest of the group.

"Mr. Matsu?" Laura cried. "Tom, Mitch, and I have been attending the Matsu School, and trying to help Nikki find you! Have you been here the whole time?"

"Not now, Laura. We don't have time," Mitch implored. "Let's get off this island first, then we'll talk."

The boys raced across the hall to open the cells on the other side. They located Emiko inside the second one. She was shocked to see them, and though she too had many questions to ask, there was no time to explain. Not now.

Not when the island was about to self-destruct.

"We have to keep moving," Mitch stressed, and they moved on to the next cell, where they found Dr. Gensai.

Dr. Gensai had barely realized he was rescued before Emiko threw herself toward her father at full force and jumped into his arms, overjoyed. Tom couldn't believe it. Vane was holding father and daughter right next to each other and they didn't even know it. Did Vane get some kind of perverse pleasure out of that?

Three more doors.

Three more chances to find their father.

The first one was empty, as was the second one.

Though Tom knew they had to hurry, he couldn't stop himself from slowing down as he approached the final door. He noticed that Mitch was doing the same. This was it. The brothers looked at each other; they tried to be brave, but the fear in their eyes was unmistakable. They each took a breath and swiped the cards.

The door swung open, and both boys held their breaths. For a second, Tom was afraid to look. Finally he forced himself to lean inside. . . .

"Dad!" Tom and Mitch called out together.

But the room was empty. They checked it anyway, but there was nothing inside. No sign that anyone had even been held in that cell. For a long moment, Tom didn't know what to do. He looked over and saw that

Mitch appeared as lost as he did. Laura's dad was there. So was Emiko's. Where was Jack Hearn?

Was he . . .

No, it was too horrible to even think about.

Tom felt a hand on his shoulder. "I'm sorry," Laura said. "I'm so sorry you're dad's not here. But you're right, we have to get out of here now. We don't have time."

"Do not fear," Mr. Ting comforted them. "Jack can take good care of himself."

Then Emiko was at the door. "Kunio did this . . . he brought me here," she said. "We have to find him."

"We know. With any luck, both Kunio and Vane will be at the bottom of the ocean by the six o'clock news," Tom said. Even as he said it, he knew there was no hope of it coming true. If anyone had a foolproof escape plan, it was Vane. But maybe Vane would leave Kunio behind. The Hearn brothers had met the young man at the Matsu School in Japan. He was bad news from the beginning, and Tom was angry with himself for not stopping him sooner. Anyone who would cheat at a skateboard race . . .

As Tom's mind drifted, Mitch tried to rally everyone together. "Okay let's book it out of here. In just under an hour, this island is going bye-bye."

"Do you have a way off the island?" Mr. Ting asked.

"Top of the line," said Tom. "Mr. Matsu has kindly

let us borrow the *Rakurai*. Thanks, by the way."

"It was my pleasure," replied Mr. Matsu, smirking.

"They're coming!" came a loud shriek from the front desk. Nadia had been standing watch.

"Do they look like they know we're here?" Tom called out.

"No, I do not think so," answered Nadia.

"How many of them are there?" Laura asked.

"Fourteen—no, fifteen," Nadia reported.

"We're going to have to fight them," Tom said.

"We're badly outnumbered," Mr. Ting replied. Then the man smiled. "I say we launch a surprise attack."

"Now that's my kind of plan!" cried Tom. "Laura, your dad's a cool dude."

"I know," Laura said, squeezing her father's hand.

"Nadia, Emiko, Dr. Gensai, stay here and wait for us to tell you it's safe," Mitch instructed. Then he turned to Tom, Laura, Mr. Ting, and Mr. Matsu. "Let's go."

The five of them raced out of the prison, screaming at the top of their lungs. There were fifteen ninjas and only five of them—assuming Mr. Matsu could fight. Well, it wouldn't be the hardest thing they would have to do that day.

Tom launched himself at the biggest one. He resisted a jumping kick. He couldn't afford to end up on the ground with a pile of Vane's goons on top of him. He struck the ninja right in the stomach with quick kick, and then spun around to snap his fist at another one.

There was confusion all around him. He caught glimpses of Tom, Laura, and the others fighting as he struggled to stay on his feet. Someone slammed his rib cage hard. Instinctively he rolled away, and when he popped up, he struck the ninja once and backed off.

Suddenly Tom realized that there were five ninjas in front of him. They advanced but didn't attack. He saw what they were doing. The other ten ninjas were keeping Mitch, Laura, and Mr. Matsu busy while the five of them clobbered him.

Even if Tom was much better than each of them individually, it was still five to one. Tom backed up. Then he realized that he was saved.

"Stop right there," he said.

"Or what?" the ninja in the center sneered.

"Or my housekeeper will clobber you," said Tom.

"Your housekeeper must be a very good one," the ninja said.

"The best, and he's a pretty good cook, too," Tom said, smiling.

"I look forward—" The ninja paused, feeling a tap on his shoulder. He turned to see who was behind him. When he did he came face-to-face with Mr. Chance. Mr. Chance nodded . . . and then clobbered him.

"The cavalry is here!" Tom shouted, loud enough so the group inside the prison would hear him too.

Then the robotic voice boomed out from the speakers attached to the sides of the facility. "THIS ISLAND WILL SELF-DESTRUCT IN FIFTY-FIVE MINUTES. ALL PERSONNEL TO THE DESIGNATED ESCAPE BOATS."

"Thanks for the reminder," Tom replied sarcastically to the voice. "I keep forgetting to check my watch."

"Funny," said Mitch. "Hey, who's that with the Chance Man?"

Next to Mr. Chance stood a man in a ninja outfit. It looked like it had once been a Black Lotus ninja uniform, but this person didn't look like a Black Lotus ninja. It looked like the owner had made some slight modifications to the Black Lotus style, and whoever he was, he seemed to be on their side. At once the strange ninja and Mr. Chance threw themselves into the thick of the fight, cornering the remaining ninjas who were battling Tom, and taking them down, one by one.

Tom saw a blur of arms and legs as he threw himself forward to join the fight. Less than a minute later, five of the ninjas were on the ground. Then he, Mr. Chance, and the new ninja ran toward Mitch, Laura, and Mr. Matsu, who had managed to lead their gang of ninjas around the corner and up to the edge of the jungle.

There were three more of Vane's goons on the ground when they got there. Now the odds were even. Tom took a deep breath.

"Boys, we must finish this quickly," Mr. Chance called out, catapulting himself in between two ninjas and slamming them both with jabs to the stomach simultaneously. Laura rushed over to make sure they stayed down.

"Mr. Chance, where have you been?" Mitch asked, striking the third ninja hard in the chest and then finishing him off with a jab to the chin. "And how did you know we were—?"

"And who's your ninja friend over there?" Tom interrupted, motioning to the new guy, who had just forced a fourth ninja to collapse in a heap on the ground.

"We will have time later to tell our tales," yelled Mr. Chance, flipping the fifth ninja upside down and keeping him down with an elbow jab to his back.

"Right, first let's get out of here," Mitch grunted, slamming a sixth ninja to the ground.

"Fine, later," Tom conceded grudgingly, thinking as he stared down the new ninja that there was something oddly familiar about him. Realizing that there was only one ninja left to fight off, Tom stepped back and prepared to perform one of his famous high kicks. "Please, allow me," he remarked to his fellow teammates as he flew high in the air and forced the final remaining goon to the ground with his sneaker.

"Well done, young sir," Mr. Chance applauded him. "Now let us move."

Mitch called to Nadia, Emiko, and Dr. Gensai, and they all raced back into the jungle, toward the *Rakurai*. As they moved, Tom managed to get a look at the slit in the ninja's mask and realized what it was about the ninja that looked so familiar. The eyes . . .

"From the subway . . . ," Mitch said, as if he was reading his brother's mind.

That was it. He was the one who had attacked them in the subway.

侍

Kunio led his small group of Black Lotus ninjas through the jungle. Vane had ordered his people to search the island, but time was running out. Kunio knew that the others wouldn't find the Hearns, however. They just didn't know the brothers like Kunio did.

People like Tom and Mitch were ridiculously

predictable. There was only one place they would go, and of course, Vane could not see it. He had his people searching the docks and any possible landing site for a ship. The island would begin coming apart soon, and Vane couldn't imagine anyone doing anything but trying to escape. He sent a group to collect the prisoners, but they of course were not prepared to meet any resistance. Only Kunio knew what was waiting for them at the prison.

Vane thought everyone in the world was like him. Kunio knew better. Kunio knew that people like Tom and Mitch were weak, and stupid enough to risk their own safety to save others. They liked to play the role of heroes; Kunio had watched them and learned. And he knew there were a lot of things that Vane could not see. He could not see Kunio's ambition, for one. Kunio's own father had lived and died a small-time crook, little more than a messenger for the real players in the Black Lotus gang. A long time ago Kunio had decided that small-time was something he would never be.

Vane had already failed in his plan to take control of the world's nuclear reactors. And he was letting the Hearn brothers slip through his fingers. The only thing Vane could salvage out of this situation was to bring in the Hearns and keep his prisoners.

But he would fail in that, too, if Kunio succeeded

in what he wanted to do. Finally Kunio would get somewhere in the Black Lotus gang . . . like his uncle had done. He wouldn't be like his father. He wouldn't be small-time.

He made his way through the jungle silently. He was close to the detention center. It wouldn't be long.

A few minutes later, he signaled his men to find cover and wait. He crept forward slowly until he could see the building . . . and the Hearns and all of Vane's prisoners standing over Vane's black ninjas.

They had not disappointed him. They were there, with the Gensais and the others. The boys had played the heroes, just as he expected them to do. Now they would pay for it. Though there were nine of them, he thought that he and his four ninjas could handle them. But he needed to be sure. He pulled his people back to the narrow stone pass a few hundred yards back. The group would have to pass through it to escape the island.

Kunio locked and loaded the assault rifle in his hands. He would be ready for them when they came.

CHAPTER 7

"How did this happen?" Vane barked, pounding his desk with his fist.

"We don't know, sir," said Baxter. The nervous man was shaking, sweat drops slowly trickling down the side of his face. He had good reason to be nervous. The current situation was intolerable.

"I want it stopped, now!" Vane yelled.

"It can't be stopped, sir," Baxter replied, beginning to sweat through his dark business suit.

"Are you telling me that in one hour, this whole place, everything I've worked for, everything I've built, is going to disappear?" said Vane, getting up and walking over to the window.

This island wasn't just his command center, it was his own world. Here, he was the master. This building was the most sophisticated communications, command, and control center on the globe. And thanks to Dr. Gensai's work on the geothermal energy system, it had almost unlimited electricity. And it was just the beginning of his new empire. There was the leverage he had because of his prisoners. From here, Vane would eventually be able to take on Rosso. And then things would really get interesting.

"Shut off the system!" Vane cried in frustration.

"We tried, but the network is down," said Baxter.

"Get it back up," Vane demanded.

"We're trying, but it looks like a virus. We suspect the Hearns," Baxter told him.

"So cut the power and the destruct system."

"We did, but it's designed to run on battery."

"Who designed that system?" Vane demanded.

"You did, sir," Baxter said. "You wanted something certain. It's a fail-safe system designed to eliminate all evidence in the event of major operational failure."

"But I'm the only one with the destruct codes, and I didn't use them," said Vane.

Baxter nodded. "The command didn't come from your terminal. Someone activated the system from one of the maintenance tunnels on the island. We don't know how, but they did it manually."

"Who? The Hearn boys?"

"No, it looks like it happened while they were still inside the communications terminal," Baxter said.

"So there's someone else running around on my island, someone who knew enough to sabotage the destruct system?"

"Yes, sir, apparently," Baxter said. The sweat was impossible to miss now. It looked as if the man had literally just stepped out of a swimming pool.

"Chance."

"Um, excuse me, sir?"

"It was Chance. Get me Chance as well. He will pay for this," Vane promised.

"There's something else, sir. We know how the Hearn brothers and the Ting girl escaped. We found four parachutes outside the compound."

"Four?" he asked.

Baxter nodded. "Nadia is missing. She may have helped them."

Vane nearly screamed in frustration and anger. "And after everything I did for her! I want her found. I want those boys found. Bring them to me in pieces if you have to. Just find them."

"Yes, sir, but there is one more thing, Mr. Vane," Baxter said.

The man hesitated, and Vane felt his anger building. "WHAT?"

"We've lost contact with the detention area. The guards aren't answering their phones. And the extraction team . . . well, we haven't heard from them."

"You lost my prisoners? Are you completely incapable of doing anything right?" Vane screamed.

"Yes, sir. I mean no, sir. I mean, sir, we'll find them, sir. I have your best ninjas on it. Now, please, let me escort you to your helicopter. We have to prepare to escape," said Baxter.

Then Vane had an idea, a remarkably simple way to motivate his people—with whom he had obviously been too soft.

"No, I don't think so," he said.

"There is a real danger, Mr. Vane," Baxter reminded his boss.

"I know, and I can find my own way to the helicopter. In the meantime, I'm putting you in charge of finding the Hearns, recovering the prisoners, and catching Chance," said Vane.

"Me, sir? I would rather stay by your side. I can't protect you unless—"

"You'll do what I tell you if you want to get off this island before it disappears into the sea," Vane said. "In fact you can tell all teams that they are not to go to their escape boats until these things are done." Vane checked his watch. "I suggest they do their jobs in less than fifty minutes. Until I hear from you that you have done what I've asked, I'm going to activate all lockout codes on escape craft. None of the staff leaves until I have what I want."

Vane escorted the man to the elevator. "I will hold the helicopter until the last possible minute. All you have to do is do your job."

"Sir, I—," Baxter sputtered.

"I suggest you hurry," said Vane.

The man nodded and headed for the elevator.

Vane turned to his computer. He transmitted the lockout codes. Fortunately the transmitter was not part of the network. Instead it was a simple radio setup. That done, he tried to log on to the network. If his incompetent staff couldn't undo whatever the Hearn boys had done, he would have to do it himself—and he knew a few hacker tricks.

As soon as he typed in his login code, a single sentence appeared on the screen. He had to look twice to make sure he had seen it correctly.

VANE IS A BUTTHEAD, the monitor said. Then it appeared again. And again, until it filled the whole screen.

Vane screamed in frustration and rage. Grabbing the monitor, he lifted it and hurled it across the room. The Hearns would pay for this. . . .

Vane walked over to a communications console and picked up a microphone.

"Attention, all Vane Enterprises personnel. This is

Julian Vane. I have suspended evacuation procedures. I need everyone to focus on the search for the three fugitives Mitchell Hearn, Thomas Hearn, and Laura Ting, as well as former staff member Nadia Petrova and our old friend Mr. Chance. In addition, the prisoners from the detention area must be recaptured. Security Chief Baxter can provide the details. I warn you that the island destruct system is still operational. You have forty-seven minutes."

侍

"He is a very bad boss," said Nadia, who was heading up the front of the group. Tom and Mitch were on either side of her.

"Sounds like the worst boss ever," Tom said.

"Now everyone knows that if they don't catch us, they go down with the island," Mitch said.

"Let's get out of here first," suggested Tom.

They tried to move as quickly as possible, but the problem was that there wasn't time for stealth. They had to move the entire group nearly a mile and a half through the jungle in less than an hour, and not everyone could keep the pace as easily as the young brothers. The prisoners were not in the best shape, having been trapped in a concrete box for weeks without proper nourishment and exercise. As Tom, Mitch, and Nadia continued to move quickly, scouting out whatever danger lay ahead, Mr. Ting, Laura, and the strange new ninja walked a few paces behind, filling out the middle. Dr. Gensai, Emiko, Mr. Matsu, and Mr. Chance rounded out the back, walking a few yards behind the front of the group. They figured that if any bad guys were coming their way, they'd see them coming from any direction.

Taking the lead, Mitch tried to remember what direction they were going in and keep them heading straight for the *Rakurai*. He saw the rocky pass up ahead and remembered it from the way in. At least they were going in the right direction.

When they were all in the center of the pass, he heard a voice shout, "Stop!"

"Run for cover!" Mitch said.

He heard the unmistakable sound of machine-gun fire. Then the ground exploded in front of him in a dozen places. Mitch skidded to a stop but was soon tackled by Mr. Chance's ally, the new ninja, and thrown to the ground. "Get down!" he screamed. "Everyone!"

"Geez," Mitch whispered, rolling out from under the ninja's grip and trying to stand. "I appreciate the concern, but that was a little creepy, dude. I hardly know you."

The new ninja quickly retreated back into the jungle to take cover under a tree. "Get back," he whispered.

Despite his misgivings about the new ninja, Mitch

jumped back at once, and Tom and Nadia followed suit.

"Stay where you are," a voice called out. Mitch realized that he recognized it.

"Kunio," he said as the teenager appeared in front of them. Kunio had an AK-47 assault rifle in his hands and two of Vane's ninjas on either side of him. "I'm so glad to see you."

They were almost twenty feet away from Kunio and the others. Attacking wouldn't just be risky, it would be suicide.

Kunio gestured with his gun. "Come on, Mr. Vane is anxious to see you."

"Well, we already met. I'll be honest, we didn't like him. There weren't any sparks," Tom said.

"Yeah, we think he's sort of a butthead," added Mitch.

"You can tell him that yourself," Kunio said.

Now it was Mitch's turn to laugh. "I already did."

"Enough games. Mr. Vane wants us to bring you to him. I forgot to mention that he doesn't care if we bring you in alive," said Kunio.

He cocked the weapon.

CHAPTER 8

At Mr. Chance's urging, Mr. Matsu, Dr. Gensai, and Emiko took cover after the gun fired, and waited in the jungle until it was quiet again. After a minute without gunfire, Mr. Chance signaled to the group at the back that it was safe to quietly move forward and check out the situation. As they marched, voices became audible.

"Stop it," cried out Mr. Matsu, once he realized who was speaking.

"Uncle Inoshiro!" Kunio exclaimed, shocked to see his uncle there, let alone traveling with these enemies. "What are you doing here? And why are you so thin?"

"Put that *thing* down," demanded Mr. Matsu.

Immediately Kunio did.

"Did you kidnap this girl?" Mr. Matsu asked, pointing back to Emiko.

"Yes," he said. "But—"

"You work for Vane, you carry that thing . . .

you shame yourself," Mr. Matsu said.

Kunio's face was burning. "Uncle, I don't understand. This is part of your plan. I just conferenced with you, on the computer—"

"What are you saying? You lie to me also? You and I have never spoken of these things. How could you think I would order you to take part in this? I have been in Vane's prison," Mr. Matsu said.

"But how?" said Kunio.

Emiko stepped forward. "You know how. That's why you brought me here. You were fooled by Vane. Because of your own actions, you made this happen."

Mitch saw that Kunio suddenly understood. He had captured Emiko so she could use her computer graphics skills to create avatars as part of Vane's plot to fool others. Vane had fooled him, too, into believing that his uncle was part of this grand plan, fooled him into thinking that he was making his uncle proud.

"What did you expect? That Vane thought you were special? That you could be trusted with the truth when others could not?" Mr. Matsu said.

For the first time since Mitch had met him, Kunio looked unsure. His world was crumbling before his eyes. He had been had.

"It was all a lie . . . ," Kunio murmured.

"A lie that cost you your honor," his uncle said.

Straightening up, Kunio pulled himself together. "Okay, it was a lie, but I don't need Vane. I'll be bigger than him eventually. Whatever happens, I won't be small-time. I won't be my father."

"Your father!" Mr. Matsu exploded.

"My father was a small-time criminal. He lived for nothing and he died for nothing," said Kunio, real pain in his face. For a second, Mitch almost felt sorry for him.

Mr. Matsu lowered his voice and he said, "My brother was a thief and a criminal. He did many shameful things and brought much dishonor to the Matsu family. But he did not terrorize young girls, and he never touched one of those." He pointed to the weapon.

"And look where it got him," Kunio protested.

Mr. Matsu shook his head. "You don't understand."

"He was beaten to death," said Kunio, near tears.

"Your father ran a small gambling operation for the Black Lotus. There was no honor in his path, but he died defending a young woman being abused by one of the Black Lotus enforcers. Whatever he did in life, he found honor in his death. And you have shamed his memory as you shame yourself and your family."

Now Mitch actually felt sorry for Kunio, who fell to his knees and cried openly. After almost a minute, he looked up at his uncle and said, "Uncle, what do I do?"

"Honor is a gift you must earn. You can start by

putting that down," his uncle told him.

Kunio threw the gun down like it was a piece of burning coal. Mitch breathed a sigh of relief. Mr. Matsu had saved them without raising a hand or striking a blow.

Just then, one of the other ninjas picked up the gun and pointed it at the group. "Mr. Vane gave us orders."

Kunio got up. "It's over," he said.

"Mr. Vane says when it's over. And it will be over when Mr. Vane has his prisoners," the ninja said.

That was when Kunio exploded into action, like a switch turned on inside him. He leaped for the ninja. Grabbing the gun with both hands, he kicked the man hard in the stomach. The ninja went flying backward.

Immediately the other three struck at Kunio from all sides. They were no match for the angry teenager. He was a blur of kicks and strikes, picking up the gun and using it alternately as a blocking tool and a club. Mitch, Tom, and Laura were no more than ten paces from the group, but before they realized what was

happening, all the ninjas were on the ground, out cold.

Kunio stood straight, his face red; once again he realized he was still holding the gun. He looked at it once in disgust and threw it aside. Mr. Matsu stepped forward, and Kunio fell into his arms. His uncle held him for a moment and said, "There is more to do. We have to get these people to safety."

Kunio nodded, and then there was a violent boom under their feet. The ground shook and Mitch nearly fell. He felt the ground shifting beneath them. He and Tom lived in New York. They had never experienced an earthquake, but Mitch recognized one when he felt it.

"What the . . . ?" Tom said.

"THIS ISLAND WILL SELF-DESTRUCT IN THIRTY-FIVE MINUTES. ALL PERSONNEL TO THE DESIGNATED ESCAPE BOATS."

Dr. Gensai stepped forward. "It is an earthquake, but it is not a natural one."

"What is it?" asked Mitch.

"It is part of the island's destruct system. This place is built on the top of a volcanic mountain. There is a large magma chamber relatively close to the surface. That is why Vane was able to build a geothermal power system—with my help, I'm afraid. I saw the plans for the self-destruct system. There will be a series of explosions, then ground wave generators will do the rest of the work.

The island will disappear, but first it will come apart. What's left will fall into the sea," Gensai explained.

"What does that mean, exactly?" Tom pressed.

"It means that the island isn't going to come apart all at once thirty-five minutes from now, but a piece at time between now and then. And while it does, we're in for a rough ride," said Mitch.

"Precisely," Dr. Gensai confirmed.

They started moving. Mr. Ting and Mr. Matsu were in surprisingly good condition. But the best Emiko and her dad were able to manage was a jog. Mitch let them set the pace. They weren't leaving anyone behind. If this was a war, they were the civilians. It was everyone else's job to protect them.

The group had covered at least a half mile when the new ninja came running out of the jungle toward them. Tom and Mitch stopped in their tracks and looked at each other in shock. They hadn't even noticed that the ninja had left; they'd been too caught up in the conversation between Kunio and his uncle.

"What's with this dude?" Tom asked Mitch. "He keeps appearing out of nowhere and then disappearing again."

"Who knows. I can't keep track of all the weird things that are happening anymore."

"There are two ninjas less than a hundred yards ahead. They're heading this way," the ninja reported.

Mitch signaled for everyone to halt.

"We could go around them," Laura suggested.

Mitch shook his head. "There's no time. Tom and I can handle this. If something goes wrong . . ." Mitch realized that he didn't have a good suggestion to offer.

"Just make sure nothing goes wrong," said Laura.

"Got it. Let's go," Tom urged, tugging at his sleeve.

"I'll come with you," the new ninja added.

They moved quickly through the jungle, keeping low. Mitch tried to be quiet, but he needed to close the distance quickly. Finally he heard a snap next to him. Looking at Tom, he saw that his brother had stepped on a stick.

"My bad," Tom said.

The Black Lotus ninjas looked over at them. That was it. They were seen. Mitch did the only thing he could think of, he raised his hand and waved.

"Dude, did you just wave to the bad guys?" Tom asked.

But it had the result he wanted. They didn't reach for their phones or call for help. Automatically the two ninjas waved back.

"Hey, you got them?" one of the Black Lotus ninjas called out. Tom and Mitch realized at once that they assumed that the new ninja, in his dark Black Lotus–style uniform, was one of them. That he had managed to capture the prisoners.

"Yeah," the new ninja called back. "Go back and tell Vane. I've already got backup."

"Right away," the Black Lotus ninja replied, and with that he and his buddy went back the way they came.

"Hey, thanks," Tom called to their new friend.

"It's the least I could do," the ninja replied.

"Hey, I think we—," Mitch started, but just then the ground shook again. It quaked so violently around them that they had to struggle to stay on their feet.

"THIS ISLAND WILL SELF-DESTRUCT IN THIRTY MINUTES. ALL PERSONNEL TO THE DESIGNATED ESCAPE BOATS."

"Perfect timing," said Tom, smiling. Mitch returned the smile until he looked up and saw at least twenty more people a few hundred yards ahead. No, not twenty. Twenty-five, maybe more. Some of them were ninjas, while some were wearing suits and ties, and others wore overalls and looked like maintenance workers.

More than one was pointing at them and shouting.

"I guess they ignored that whole, 'I don't need backup' speech, huh?" Mitch said, turning to the new ninja.

At once, the three turned and ran back toward the rest of the group. "We've got trouble," Mitch announced.

"What happened?" asked Laura.

"Mitch waved at them," Tom said.

Mitch shot him a look and said, "Hey, it worked.

But now we have to get out of here."

"There's nowhere to go. Even if we could get away, we have to go straight through or we'll never make the boat in time," Laura said.

"How many are there?" asked Kunio.

"All of them, I think," Tom answered.

"He's right. It's not just ninjas, it looks like everybody, and they'll be here very soon," Mitch said.

"We can fight," said Mr. Ting.

"Listen, we're good, don't get me wrong, but we'll lose. There are just too many of them," Tom replied.

"There is still dignity in fighting a losing battle for a just cause," Mr. Ting assured them.

Had they run out of options? No, they still had options. The problem was that all of them were bad.

Tom smiled. "The odds are against us. The island's coming apart around us. What's not to love? All right, let's go get 'em. We're running low on time."

Mitch smiled back. Then Laura did too. But Mr. Chance looked sick. No doubt he was worried about them.

"Wait," said Kunio. Everyone turned to look at him. "There is another way, but I don't think you're going to like it."

"I've yet to like anything that's happened on this forsaken island," Tom reminded him. "Try me."

CHAPTER 9

"There are tunnels. They were built during the war. Vane used them to run power cables and store equipment. There's an entrance nearby," Kunio explained.

"But if we're underground when one of the quakes hits . . . ," Laura said.

"I told you that you wouldn't like it," said Kunio.

"It's our only chance. Where's the entrance?" Mitch asked. He realized that he had just put their lives in Kunio's hands, but it felt like the right thing to do.

Kunio led them to a small tunnel entrance. He opened the door. "Uncle, we can take the lead." Kunio's uncle nodded and they stepped inside.

Mitch was glad to see that there were lights inside. Otherwise this would have been completely impossible . . . instead of *practically* impossible.

"We'll back you up," said Tom.

"We will take the rear," Mr. Ting said.

They were off. Mitch had to crouch to get inside the door. Once he was inside, he could stand, which made traveling easier. The tunnel was just wide enough for two people to stand side by side.

"If the search party sees us going in, this is going to get much harder," Tom said.

A few steps later, he heard shouting behind them.

"I think it just got harder," said Mitch.

"They're behind us," Tom called ahead to Kunio and Mr. Matsu.

"They're in front of us too," Kunio yelled. Then he dashed ahead. There were shouts and grunts and dust. A few seconds later, there were two ninjas on the ground.

"Come on," Kunio said.

Mitch and Tom raced forward, feeling Mr. Chance and the new ninja on their heels. They reached an opening. The tunnel connected to a chamber that was at least twenty feet across.

"Wait, I have an idea," Mitch called ahead.

Kunio and Mr. Matsu stopped and turned. "Let's see if we can hold them up behind us a bit," said Mitch. He pointed to the large spools of electric cable and crates of equipment. They waited until the Gensais, the Tings, and Nadia entered the chamber, then they

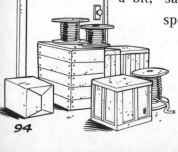

all threw as many things as they could into the narrow tunnel.

"That should hold them off," Mitch said.

At that exact moment, a door they hadn't seen opened up on one of the chamber's far walls. A Black Lotus ninja stepped through and headed straight for them. Before anyone could react, the new ninja was on the goon, who went down quickly. So did the next one.

Then the new ninja slammed the door shut. Mitch tossed a crate in front of it. Tom did the same. Less than a minute later, there was a pile of boxes and equipment blocking the door.

"How are we doing on time?" Kunio asked.

"You don't want to know," replied Mitch.

"Right," Kunio said, turning to race ahead.

Twice more, there was fighting in front of them. Then Kunio called out, "Coming toward you."

Two people in street clothes came flying back while the brothers heard the sound of more fighting up ahead. Mitch and Tom took out the two men and then stepped over two more who lay on the ground.

Mitch gave up trying to calculate where they were. It seemed like they had made a lot of progress, but it was hard to say. Finally they reached another chamber. Kunio and Mr. Matsu were waiting there, and once again, they let the others collect inside. There were only a few crates this time, but they tossed them into the tunnel behind them.

"That will slow them down at least," Tom said.

"There's still a lot of them to slow down," said Laura. "I'd guess at least fifteen, maybe twenty."

Kunio told the others, "The exit is maybe a hundred and fifty yards ahead."

"Great, let's go," Tom said.

"You go on ahead," said Kunio.

"What do you mean?" Laura asked.

"I mean that I will stay to make sure you are not followed," Kunio said.

"*We* will stay," corrected his uncle. Kunio looked at him, and something passed between them.

"We're *all* going," Tom said.

"No," Kunio stated. His tone was final. And his voice sounded much older. "In a narrow tunnel, their numbers work against them. In the open it will be different. They will chase us, separate us, and pick us off one at a time. If we run, you know that is what will happen."

"Then what happens to you?" Laura asked.

"We'll follow when the time is right," said Kunio.

"No, you won't. And you don't intend to," Laura said.

Kunio shook his head. "It is the only way. Let me do this. I have shamed myself and shamed my family. This may be the only moment I have to do something good. Let me have it."

The chamber was silent. Mitch couldn't believe his ears. Yet he understood. It made sense. In fact it might be the only way to save what was left of the mission.

"Not in a million years," he said.

"Yeah, forget it," Tom agreed.

"We all stay, or we all go," said Laura.

"We've got time. We can all still make it, right, Mitch?" Tom said.

Mitch checked his watch. "Um . . . sure," he answered.

"You're lying," Kunio said, smiling.

Before Mitch could reply, he felt a hand on his shoulder. It was Mr. Chance. "Boys. You cannot win every battle. The world is not black-and-white. There are shades of gray in everything. And sometimes you have to accept an incomplete victory. Better that than a defeat."

Mr. Matsu stepped forward and said, "It is our way. It is the way of the Thunderbolt Clan. The way of the samurai."

"Well, it's not *our* way. It's not the way we do things back in New York," Tom protested.

"Yeah, we don't leave people behind," Mitch said. "That's not how our father raised us." Mitch thought about their dad. Laura had found hers. Emiko had hers.

Where was theirs? Mitch had no idea. He did know one thing: If Mitch and Tom ever saw their dad again, there was only one way they could face him.

Just then, they heard a crash. They turned to see their new friend, the strange ninja, face first on the ground, tangled in one of the electric cords. "Don't worry about me. I just wasn't paying attention, that's all."

Mitch and Tom exchanged looks. Tom was sure he'd caught the new ninja smirking. "That guy is so weird," Tom remarked.

"Emiko, Dr. Gensai, Nadia, you go on ahead," said Mitch, getting back to business.

"No, thank you," Dr. Gensai said. "You all have done so much for me and my daughter. I want to help." He picked up what looked like an old torch that was hanging on the wall. He swung it like a club.

Emiko stood with her father. "Me too. I'm stronger than I look."

"Nadia, you have to get out of here—"

"No," she said. "I don't think so. I think I'll make up my own mind, thank you. I worked for Vane. I won't be taking orders from anyone for a long time."

Kunio sighed.

"They're coming," said Laura.

"Wait, I've got a plan," Tom said. "Grab me that wire." He pointed to a small spool on the ground. As Mitch did,

Tom picked up two short posts from the tunnel floor. Mitch understood, and the brothers quickly set a trap by running wire across the entrance, just a few inches off the ground.

They were just in time. Mitch saw people coming. Because the tunnel was so narrow, he could see only a few of them. There was no way to estimate how many were behind them.

Kunio looked at their trap and smiled. "That'll never work."

Tom smiled back and said, "Wanna bet?"

Two of Vane's ninjas raced for them at full speed.

"Sorry, but you're going down!" Tom called.

A second later their feet hit the wire, and Tom was right. They went down hard. A few blows later and they stayed down. Then two more came, then two more. Some were ninjas, some were not. All of them went down.

In less than five minutes, they stopped coming. Most of them were on the ground. Others, he saw, simply ran the other way.

"Will you go *now*?" said Kunio.

At that moment there was an explosion underfoot. Then the walls and floor were shaking. This time the sound was deafening.

"Now we're *all* going," Mitch shouted. "Everyone out."

CHAPTER 10

Tom and Mitch pushed everyone into the tunnel and toward the exit. Mr. Chance took the lead, and the boys intended to pick up the rear. However, they found someone behind them, pushing them forward.

Tom was surprised to see that it was the new ninja. Everyone got outside safely.

Maybe "safely" isn't the word, Tom thought. On the outside, it looked like the world was coming apart. The ground was shaking, and he could see cracks opening up in the earth nearby.

"THIS ISLAND WILL SELF-DESTRUCT IN FIFTEEN MINUTES. ALL PERSONNEL TO THE DESIGNATED ESCAPE BOATS."

"Run, keep moving forward," he shouted.

Up ahead, he saw it, the *Rakurai*, less than three hundred yards away. It was attached to a dock. But those three hundred yards might as well have been a mile. Tom ran anyway. He did his best to keep his eye on the others. They couldn't lose anyone, not now. Not after they had come this far.

The ground rumbled and shook. Nevertheless they somehow made it to the dock. No one tried to stop them. No one seemed to be left.

The dock and the ship seemed deserted. As they ran, the ground settled down.

"Let's move now," Mitch said.

Mr. Chance was first up the gangplank, and then he helped the others. Finally it was Mitch and Tom's turn, with the new ninja following right behind them.

When they were all onboard, the boys ran for the mooring lines. While they were busy trying to untie the boat from the dock, they heard a commotion behind them. When Tom turned, Mr. Chance and the new ninja were tumbling down the gangplank. They hit the dock, got up . . . and started fighting.

"Mr. Chance!" Tom and Mitch screamed together.

The butler ignored him. The new ninja forced Mr. Chance backward. Finally he had to leap onto the shore. The new ninja stayed on him.

The boys ran toward the gangplank, prepared to come to Mr. Chance's defense, when they heard a rumble that they recognized. The brothers saw the island shake in front of them as the ship pitched back and forth. They had to hang on to the railing to keep from going over the side.

Immediately the ship started to move away from the shore. Tom saw the danger. Even if Chance won the fight, he was stuck on an island that was coming apart. "Captain, we need to get this bucket started and get back there. We have to rescue Mr. Chance."

"I'm on it," Mitch said, racing for the bridge.

"Kunio, get everyone inside and tell them to hang on," said Tom.

The young man nodded and started helping the others into the ship. Looking back to the shore, Tom saw that the fight was turning nasty.

The new ninja was extremely aggressive. He looked like he was fighting angry. And Mitch had seen Mr. Chance fight before, but never like this. Whatever was going on, Tom was sure of one thing: Only one of these two men would walk away from this fight.

He heard Mitch shouting from the bridge and Laura answering him. What he didn't hear were the ship's engines. And they were drifting farther away from the island.

That was when Tom saw the first lava flow. It was at least a hundred yards away from the fighting men, but Tom was worried. Then he saw lava pop up suddenly from a point on the shoreline nearby. It made contact with the water, which began to bubble and steam almost immediately. This was it. The island was actually coming apart!

In his worried state, Tom began to think irrationally. "I'm jumping off. I have to help him!" he cried.

"Are you crazy?" Laura called out, running to stop him. "That's molten lava down there. You can't save him. There's nothing you can do, and jumping into that water is just going to get you hurt, or worse. Mr. Chance is a strong fighter. He can take care of himself."

Tom didn't answer, but the fact that he was still standing there told Laura he knew she was right.

Tom knew Mr. Chance didn't have much time left. "Mitch!" he shouted.

"Got it," his brother shouted back. Then the ship came to life. Tom could hear engines roar. He also felt their vibration in his feet.

"Get us closer! I've got to get one line on the dock! The water is boiling. He'll never make it if we can't get right up to the dock!"

Somehow Mitch got the ship under control in the choppy seas. The *Rakurai* was built for speed, not for maneuvering in rough water. But Mitch was managing. They inched closer and closer. The gangplank was now holding a few feet away from the dock. It would have to be close enough.

Mr. Chance and the new ninja continued to battle each other. Tom could not believe that they were still fighting at such intensity. They looked like two masters fighting for their lives. I guess they are, Tom thought.

There was lava all around them now. Even if the two fighters could keep it up indefinitely, the island would not last much longer. Mr. Chance launched an aggressive series of attacks that pushed the ninja back. Then he did something that shocked Tom more than anything else so far. Mr. Chance pulled out a knife from under his sleeve.

Suddenly the new ninja was wary. He gave Mr. Chance a lot of room. Mr. Chance didn't hesitate. He attacked, slashing out at the ninja. But instead of ducking or pulling back, the ninja leaned in. As a result, Mr. Chance slashed him in the left arm. But the ninja struck with his right. He caught Mr. Chance right in the face. Their butler staggered back. The new ninja attacked again, this time grabbing the knife. Recovering quickly, Mr. Chance launched himself forward. The men grappled and went down to the ground.

Tom didn't see the knife when they got up. But he did see that Mr. Chance had a deep gash running down the left side of his face.

Then the ninja adopted a ready stance and did something strange. It was subtle, but something that Tom immediately recognized. The ninja went up slightly onto the balls of his feet before his attack. Then he let loose a devastating kick that caught Mr. Chance directly in the chest.

Once again Tom realized there was something familiar about this new ninja. He had seen that move before. In the subway station, when the ninja had attacked him and Mitch. A few moments after was when they had met Laura for the first time. It was also sort of their first introduction to the world of the R.O.N.I.N.

The new ninja didn't even look to see if Mr. Chance was getting up. Instead he turned and ran for the *Rakurai*, which was slowly drifting away from the shaking dock. Hitting the dock at full speed, the ninja launched himself onto the deck.

Tom could not help but be impressed by the jump. The ninja just caught the edge of the gangplank with his feet, sprang forward, then raced up the plank and onto the ship. A moment later he was standing less than five feet from Tom.

Too shocked to move, Tom just stared at the ninja for a moment. Then the boat shook. Tom watched as the dock disintegrated.

Mr. Chance was nowhere in sight.

Suddenly the cracks in the ground of the island were huge. Some of them had filled with water. Others were running with boiling lava. And then something exploded out of the top of the volcano. Rocks flew through the air around them.

The *Rakurai* started to pull away from the island. Tom knew that Mitch was doing the only thing he could. He was getting them out of there.

The electronic warning rang out once more from the speakers stationed on the outer walls of all of Vane's facilities and outstations. "THIS ISLAND WILL SELF-DESTRUCT IN FIVE MINUTES. ALL PERSONNEL TO THE DESIGNATED ESCAPE BOATS."

Just a few hundred yards away, the sea was much calmer. Tom watched as the whole island shook. He could see Vane's Space Needle sway back and forth. Pieces of its center support fell off. Large pieces. Then the whole thing leaned heavily in one direction . . . and kept falling.

Vane's plans were evil . . . and insane, but Tom found himself sorry to see that giant structure fall. And fall it did. . . .

For a moment time seemed to slow. For just a second, it looked like the building would sway back into position. Then something snapped with a loud boom. The support broke and the giant saucer fell. Even from here and with the roar of the shaking earth, Tom heard the crash. The saucer exploded into a thousand pieces as it hit the jungle floor.

Suddenly Mitch was next to him.

"Give us one reason we shouldn't throw you overboard," Mitch called out to the ninja from the other side of the boat. Tom realized that he had been in a bit of a trance and snapped back to reality. As he started walking toward the ninja, he also noticed that Mr. Chance was still nowhere to be seen.

"Just give me a few minutes; I can explain everything. I promise I won't disappoint you," the ninja said. For the first time since the ninja had arrived on the island, he spoke enough for Tom to really hear his voice. And there was something about his voice . . . something very strange.

And very familiar.

"We've heard that one before. Not a chance. You're going over!" Mitch screamed, and began running toward the ninja, preparing to take revenge.

"Look, boys, I really don't want to have to ground you," the ninja called out, pulling off his hood and mask.

"Dad!" Mitch and Tom shouted together, stopping in their tracks.

Jack Hearn smiled at his sons. "I told you I wouldn't disappoint you."

DYLAN SPROUSE AND COLE SPROUSE ARE TWO OF HOLLYWOOD'S MOST EMINENT RISING STARS.

Dylan and Cole were born in Arezzo, Italy, and currently reside in Los Angeles, California. Named for the jazz singer and pianist Nat King Cole, Cole's list of favorites includes math, the color blue, and animals. He also enjoys video games and all types of sports, including motocross, snowboarding, and surfing. Dylan, named after the poet Dylan Thomas, is very close to his brother and also has a great love of animals and video games. He enjoys science, the Los Angeles Lakers, and the color orange. He's a sports enthusiast and especially loves motocross, snowboarding, surfing, and basketball.

Cole and Dylan made their acting debuts on the big screen in *Big Daddy*, opposite Adam Sandler. Both also starred in *The Astronaut's Wife*, *Master of Disguise*, and *Eight Crazy Nights*. On television Cole and Dylan established themselves in the critically acclaimed ABC comedy series *Grace Under Fire* and eventually went on to star in NBC's *Friends* as David Schwimmer's son, Ben Geller.

Dylan and Cole currently star as the introspective Cody Martin and the mischievous Zack Martin, respectively, in the Disney Channel's amazingly successful sitcom *The Suite Life of Zack and Cody*, playing separate roles for the first time. Ranked number one in its time slot against all basic cable shows, *The Suite Life* is now one of the Disney Channel's top shows and is rapidly gaining worldwide success.

In September 2005 the Sprouses partnered with Dualstar Entertainment Group to launch the Sprouse Bros. brand, the only young men's lifestyle brand designed by boys for boys. The brand includes *Sprouse Bros. 47 R.O.N.I.N.*, an apparel collection, an online fan club, mobile content, a DVD series in development, and lots more in the works!

LOOK FOR THESE OTHER SPROUSE BROS. 47 R.O.N.I.N. BOOKS!

EPISODE #1: THE REVELATION

EPISODE #2: THE SHOWDOWN

EPISODE #3: THE GETAWAY

EPISODE #4: THE SIEGE

AND DON'T FORGET TO CHECK OUT
EPISODE #6: THE COMEBACK,
COMING SOON TO STORES NEAR YOU!

SPROUSE BROS

CHECK OUT

sprousebros.com

FOR GOOD TIMES, SWEET
CONTESTS AND THE LATEST
ON DYLAN, COLE AND THE
SPROUSE BROS BRAND!

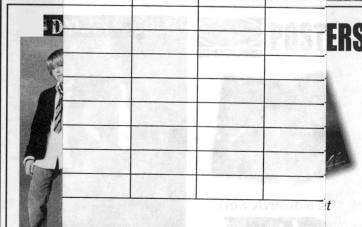
DATE DUE
